T0128942

# ANGEL WINGS

LaKecia
Rodriguez

authorHOUSE®

*AuthorHouse™*
*1663 Liberty Drive*
*Bloomington, IN 47403*
*www.authorhouse.com*
*Phone: 1 (800) 839-8640*

*Published by AuthorHouse 12/14/2017*

*ISBN: 978-1-5462-2001-5 (sc)*
*ISBN: 978-1-5462-2000-8 (e)*

Since the beginning of time there has been a war….a war between right and wrong, good versus bad, and worse yet the very forces of heaven and the good it entails versus the evil that consumes each and every one of us at one point of time or another. What saves us from making the conscious choice of following a path of righteousness sometimes is not our choice—but our calling.

FIVE YEARS AGO…..

"I must admit brother that you telling me about this town and the people here has been very beneficial to me."

"I thought that you would like the quiet and calm here. Better than when you were in the big city with all the people that used you there."

Fannie Gray liked the big city, and the needs of the greedy, self-absorbed people who came to her for her various services. They came, all statuses asking for everything from fame to riches, sexual prowess to revenge. She satisfied all requests brought to her. It wasn't until she ran across a big businessman in the city that things got fuzzy. She had did multiple favors for him to triple his riches and provide extra protection from law enforcement for him. When she turned down his money and asked for proper payment was when she was ran out of town, barely escaping with her life. They didn't understand that the more favors that they asked her the higher the price. Their money wasn't enough to cover the lives that were ruined. She was a death dealer, and the deeper the sin the more blood it required her to provide to stay powerful as she was. Their money paled in comparison to the divine power she held—she hated those men that wanted power just to destroy someone else.

So it was left up to her to go after her payment; her revenge. The businessman's son was murdered—and quite grisly—and his body left at his father's front gate. Irate, the businessman found out that it was her and placed a contract out for her life—nothing that Fannie worried about, being powerful as she was—that she couldn't have gotten rid of all of them. She would have to bide her time, but before being ran out of town she would give law enforcement what they needed to know to 'investigate' some of the businessman's dealings. He was eventually arrested and most of the material goods he had that his wife didn't get went to the government for the millions he had scammed people and gotten from his business partners. She took her leave instead of drawing more attention to herself. Maybe a small town would be a solution to her problems.

When her brother invited her to the small town outside Newark, he lived in for a rest away from the big city. He had always told her that she should have come and stayed with him and settle down. Her husband wanted to live quietly in a small town, but Fannie wanted the big life, complete with the money and nice houses. Her husband never suspected that she dabbled in black magic, and if he did he never made mention of it. But before she got into some of her contracts with the big businessmen that she knew he died, and she never shed a tear. It wasn't until she moved back to the small city that her brother knew that he had passed on, and by that time he had been gone over a year.

Once she settled in the small town her brother lived in it wasn't long before she made her 'services' available to the townsfolk. Her services always came with the disclaimer that the payment must be made, and money wasn't always the payment. Most of the townsfolk gave proper payment, or was careful about what they asked of her. Some stayed away from her altogether. When her brother Marlon came to her he wanted many things. The first thing he asked was for his son to be accepted into the military and them not being able to find out that he had been in trouble with the law. Then after that he wanted his son to pass his exams for he could bring more prestige to the family.

He paid her the money she asked for, for his son would repay him for his 'help'. When his other son wanted to get into med school and he was applying for a scholarship and his grades and paper had to be up to snuff, she swayed the judgment panel for him to get in. She also got a big sum of money from him for those services also. She lived quite well on the outskirts of town, and advised many of the townspeople. She even had a loyal following. It wasn't until Grace Carroll came into town that Fannie Gray became concerned about her power being threatened.

Grace Carroll came to the town not by choice. She had run into a bad run of luck, her husband had been killed, and the money from his insurance and other funds was running out. It was hard to keep everything together in a big city, so she moved to a small town to slow down the way her money was going. Once there she got two jobs to support herself and her daughter, and had enough money to buy a house flat out. She worked day and night to provide for her and Angelica, and almost immediately Fannie Gray sensed something in Grace Carroll that made her hate her on sight. Just like she helped people with their needs, so did Grace, but from a good point of view, not asking for payment. Fannie saw Grace's good deeds as a threat to her, and that threat had to be eliminated.

People began to talk, wondering why Fannie had taxed them so hard for her services, when Grace didn't. Fannie wasn't going to take that disrespect from her followers or the townspeople that asked her for her services. When she saw that her services wasn't as popular as before then she declared war against Grace Carroll, and wouldn't stop until she saw her dead. Their war would last three years with her questionable death. She thought that she had dealt with her problem—it only was delayed. Everybody has a price to pay.

For a while things went back to normal. Then Marlon came to Fannie again, this time with a different request. He wanted his now teenage daughter's friend.

Fannie looked at him and laughed. "What is it you want from that girl? You should ask for me to fix your wife don't you think?"

"I want my daughter's friend Anastasia. I want her body."

"Ah, I see. I can make your wife more intimate with you."

"Are you hard of hearing? I don't want my wife. I want my daughter's friend Anastasia. Are you going to give me her or not?"

"And my payment? Are you willing to give it?"

"Yes, I will give you the usual amount."

"Money does not pay for that type of favor. You know that. Are you willing to pay the price for what you truly want?"

"What is the payment for what I desire?"

"Blood. You want that young girl to want you, and you also want to go further than that. Am I correct?"

Enraged, Marlon looked at her, "Are you going to do it or what? You know that you have competition! You won't do it I'll lie to Grace Carroll and get her to give me the girl. Your choice."

Fannie laughed at Marlon. "Are you daring me? Grace Carroll is no match for me. She's not even on my caliber for power. But if you want to use her, have fun with that. She doesn't do the same magic that I do and you know that."

"You're just threatened by her pretty face. Right? No matter. Everyone in town knows about how much you hate the woman. But I'm not concerned about that, all I want is my request. If you can't do it, I will get what I want."

"Are you going to pay me what I ask?"

"Sure, give me what I want!!"

"As long as I get my payment!"

Marlon watched as Fannie prepared a potion for him. For months he had watched his daughter bring in her friends Angelica and Anastasia. He didn't care too much for Angelica, and didn't see why his daughter even befriended her—maybe she did it out of pity. Now Anastasia had promise. She was already too shapely for a girl her age, and had many men of the town fantasizing about sleeping with her. Marlon wouldn't fantasize, he would make it reality. It didn't matter that he was good friends with her father, he was going to make a woman out of her before the other men would taint her.

When his daughter asked could she come over he permitted it. He would use this time to see if Fannie's potion worked or no. He didn't care about her bullshit about payment, he wouldn't pay her with blood, but money as he usually did. Who did she think she was talking to about blood anyway? She provided a service, and she was going to get what he decided was good enough for her to have. If it wasn't for him she'd never be as well off here as she was. He readied himself for Anastasia's arrival. He tried not to seem too excited for he didn't want his wife to find him useless things to do to keep him away from seeing the girl.

He remembered back to the first time his daughter brought her home. Anastasia seemed to develop overnight, and much faster than his daughter, which made him wonder was something going on with her or was she a virgin like her daughter teased her about. If she was, she would lose it to him. The memory that burned in his mind was when her and his daughter were in the garage getting something for her mother. Anastasia had stopped by their car, not knowing that he was fixing it. He slowly rolled from under the car to see her undersides—he laid there looking at her hairless crotch and lacy panties. He smelled her scent. He knew then that he wanted her.

He slowly eased back under the car until they left the garage, and got from under the car and into the car. He had a raging hard-on, and relived himself in the car. At first he felt guilty, he had a wife that would have given him sex anytime he wanted. But over the years she had become less appealing. He had cheated on her before, always dealing with ladies at the bars or prostitutes for what he wanted in sex. He had met up with some women that redefined his tastes in sex. When he tried what he learned on his wife, she pushed him away stating that they never did that before and wouldn't entertain it.

She knew from that he had been cheating, and stopped sleeping with him unprotected, which he found to be an insult. She went to Fannie after seeing that he was cheating and asked for her help, unknowing that he had asked for to be able to sleep around. She loved her husband, and didn't want him sleeping around. Fannie found all of the confusion delightful and profitable. She felt sorry for her and gave her potion for free. She only hoped that Marlon would change his ways, but didn't see that happening. He had moved on from his wife to younger pursuits. When he would be found out then what would he do?

That night while his wife and daughter slept he couldn't sleep. He went to the kitchen to get something to drink. He was agitated with Anastasia being in the house and him not being able to have her. He had placed the potion in her drink earlier and since she hadn't acted interested had decided that Fannie had duped him. He was shaken out of his thought by Anastasia coming down into the kitchen for a drink. He turned to see her in a t-shirt and panties. Her nipples were pointy. She stopped when she saw Marlon in the kitchen.

"Did I wake you?"

"No."

He looked at her as she walked to the fridge to get some more to drink. He walked behind her. She felt his hardness and shimmied away from him. He liked the art of the chase, and let her move out of the kitchen. She tried to go back up the stairs but he stopped chasing her after seeing how nervous he made her. He needed for her to come away from the stairs. He thought quickly. "Your parents left some money for you to go to whatever you and my daughter were going tomorrow. Let me give it to you."

He walked into the den, she slowly followed. Once by the door he snatched her in. It was there he took her virginity, at first with her being resistant. After her blood got to flowing the potion took effect and had her two more times after that. After their romp they cleaned up, and he gave her the money (his money), and they crept back into their beds. Every chance he would get from that time on they would have sex. Enraged at how he went back on his payment Fannie got what she desired. Since Marlon didn't want to pay her correctly she would take his son. She would not be denied her payment. Marlon was at home with his wife when the knock came on the door. She walked to the door and he was shook up at his wife's scream. He ran out to the door with his revolver.

"What the hell is going on?"

His wife was there on her knees sobbing with the paper in her hand. The military officer tried to console her while defusing the situation. "I'm sorry Mr. Peterson, your son has been killed in the line of duty." His wife screamed and cried again. He looked at the man, then his wife and nodded his head. After they left and he helped his wife to the couch he shook his head in disbelief. His son dead? How? He did he get killed? He never saw combat, he was intelligence, an inside man. He had to know. He went to Fannie for help. She would help him get through the red tape.

Fannie would listen to Marlon and his wife's woes. While she sympathized with Marlon's wife, she didn't have any on Marlon. His son was her payment, and her way to let him know that his requests were now not payable by money. She consoled his wife, and listened to her request. She wanted her to tell her about her husband's discretions, but thought against it. After his wife left, she waited for Marlon to come. She wouldn't wait for long. She had just finished talking with some of her followers about Grace Carroll and her daughter. She wanted her dead and was making moves for that to happen.

Marlon came in in a huff. "I need you to help me find out what happened to my son."

She looked at him and laughed. "You're on time I can give you that. Your wife wants the same thing. Do you talk to her anymore? Or is she your ex-wife?"

He slapped Fannie across the face. "Listen witch, I need to know what happened to my son, not for you to be cute about what I do with my life! Give me clearance to find out what the military isn't telling us!"

"There's nothing to tell. He was at the wrong place at the wrong time. Someone else was supposed to be there. He took that persons place unknowingly. Twist of fate. You will be paid quite well for his death that should help you. Proper payment for me, don't you think?"

Marlon slapped Fannie across the room and was about to slap her again but stopped. He looked at her. He didn't need for her to have a change of attitude. It was through her that he was having all the sex he wanted with his daughter's friend and that he did it under the veil of secrecy. If Weber knew that he had been sleeping with his daughter he would have his head. Over the months they had gotten sloppy, and she had gotten pregnant, but he took care of that as well using Fannie again for to alter Anastasia's memory of it. He left to deal with his wife and the burial of his son. But Fannie wasn't through. How dare he put his hands on her! She would take whole family if she had to. He didn't know who he was messing with!!

The first attack from Fannie to Grace Carroll came with two intruders in her home. Grace Carroll fought off the attackers that came into her home. Two of them caught bullets dead on. She had now known that Fannie was out to get her. She had told her to move out of her 'territory' and to find her own. She was told that two people of their powers can't live in peace with each other. She claimed the whole town and its people as hers, and she would get rid of her even if that meant to take the thing closest to her. Once she saw that Grace wasn't backing down she would do just that. But before that Marlon had to be taught a lesson. You don't disrespect those who help you over your bridges. Fannie would take his last son. That would teach him about where to put his hands. Eight months after they buried their oldest son they would bury their remaining son.

Grace tried to warn the Petersons about dealing with her, as she did other people of the town. They all wanted what she was giving-- they wanted instant fame, money, sexual favors, and anything else material they could get without working for it. Some things that she knew were illegal that some of the townspeople were asking for. More bodies of the homeless and the prostitutes were found dead. Nobody made much a deal about it. Grace began to pray and make safeguards for her daughter. She would sew things in her clothes, or would have her take something for protection. What other way would she keep her daughter safe from what was going on in the town?

During this time Grace was visited by an older woman who

had told her of the history of the town. She urged her to protect her daughter, and watch who she allowed her to associate with. She entrusted seven books to her, which she tried to open and read them, but didn't understood what was written in them. When she asked the other women about the woman visitor, they all looked at her like she lost her mind. Only after she went to the local city hall asking about where the woman stayed that she was told that the woman had died decades ago.

Devastated at the loss of another son Mrs. Peterson very seldom interacted with the people of the town. She clung very close to their remaining child Alexandra, fearing that she too would die. If only she knew that it all was her husband's fault that her sons were gone. If only she knew all her husband had did behind her back, or the pacts that he made with Fannie. But she didn't know. Her marriage to Marlon was just a sham. She heard the murmurs of Marlon's dealings with prostitutes. All she had left was the love that she had for her daughter and her daughter's life.

Marlon became strict on Alex after her brother's death. She was the average teenager—popular and into everything. He knew that she was sexually active (and through people of the town well used). She would buck against her dad every chance she would get. She tired of her mother altogether. It wasn't until Fannie would invite her out to her home for her to be 'serviced' that Fannie would slip up. When the men became uncontrollable shots rang out four bullets hitting Fannie. Two in her chest, one in her stomach, and the final one in her back. As she laid dying she uttered a final curse—*Vengeance on Marlon and his bloodline and curses on those that shot me! Ultimate vengeance on the Carroll clan!* When three of the men saw that she was dead they cleaned up the area. She was buried in the forest by her house and the house locked down.

FIVE YEARS LATER.....

All I remember about the accident was bits and pieces. Crunching of metal. Lights. Feeling the wind. Being shaken around. Muffled voices. What's going on? I can't see anything! Oh my God, I'm blind!

Where am I? Where are my girlfriends? I don't hear them. Where am I being taken? I pass back into unconsciousness.

"I don't know how she survived", Lance said to Harry. "She should have been dead too."

"Lord works in mysterious ways. Just a shame how this accident happened. Police think the driver was drunk." Harry replied.

"The driver, huh?"

"Whatever she hit or whatever hit her threw her like a football. She's at least 20 feet from here."

"Well at least she's not as bad off as the girl on the passenger side. Head nearly cut off. Bled out before help could get through to her. All of them too young for this to happen to them. The fire did a number on the second one."

"I hate to be the police officer that has to tell the families of these girls about this accident. The news is going to be devastating! Especially since the only one that survived should have gotten it the worst. Somebody must been praying for that girl." Harry said.

"There you go with that religious stuff again. Better not let ol' Patton hear you talking like that. He'd fire you and boot you so far you'll feel like that girl 25 yards away. Another loss for the Peterson household. This was their last child."

But Harry knew. As he walked off from Lance he knew. That girl should have died. He saw it before, many years ago when he was young. He just hoped that the girl was just lucky. As he went back to the fire engine he couldn't shake the feeling that this girl would cross his path again.

The call broke the silence of the night. Olive Webster went to answer the phone. "Hello?"

"May I speak to Mr. or Mrs. Webster?"

"This is Mrs. Webster."

"Mrs. Webster, there's been an accident." Olive began screaming, having heard on the news of an auto accident. Her scream scared Richard out of a sound sleep. He ran to where she was and grabbed the phone from her. "Hello? Who is this?"

"Mr. Webster this is Officer Daily from Newark police. Your daughter has been involved in an accident."

"What?! Where? Is she ok?"

"I'm sorry."

"What do you mean, you're sorry? Where is my daughter?"

"She's deceased. I will need for you to come to the morgue to identify her body."

Mr. Webster fell silent. He looked at his wife. He looked back at the phone and hung it up. His wife looked to him for clarity. "Rich, is our daughter…..?"

He held her close, almost squeezing her to death. She pulled away to see the tears forming in her husband's eyes. The last time she remembered him crying was at his mother's funeral. A chill fell over her body. She wanted to hear it. "Is Anastasia ok?"

"She's gone." He looked at her with tears flowing. "She's gone." Olive fainted.

Eric Daily loved his job being a policeman for the most part. But this was the part he hated—telling loved ones that their son or daughter, mother or father was killed in an accident. He knew that the women always took it hardest, followed by the men just becoming numb at the loss. As he went to the house of Nancy and Marlon Peterson he felt laden with the heavy burden of telling them that their daughter had passed away. He sighed, not wanting to be in the position. He pulled up outside of the Peterson's to see Mrs. Peterson taking her blanket off the swing on their front porch. She saw him and waved, wondering what he was doing so far out.

She walked toward him with her blanket in hand. She offered him some coffee, which he declined. "What brings you here, Eric?"

"I need to talk to you and Marlon."

"Marlon! Marlon! Deaf man!"

"What!"

"Eric Daily's down here, needs to talk to us."

"He can tell you! My game's on."

"That man!!"

"Mr. Peterson please come down. This is about Alex."

Eric heard the footsteps coming to where they were standing. Annoyed he looked at Eric Daily like he really messed up his TV time. "Mrs. Mr. Peterson, there's been an accident."

He looked at Eric. "What Alex do this time? Where is my car? Was she driving?"

"Apparently so."

"Was she drinking? Did smell you it on her?"

"I don't think you understand Mr. Peterson."

"You said that Alex was drinking while driving. How much is it going to cost me to get her out this time?"

"Mr. Peterson, Alex is dead."

Mr. Peterson stood there in disbelief; his wife was already in tears. He looked at Eric as if he was playing a joke.

"C'mon, Eric. That's a mean thing to say about Alex. I know you two like to play practical jokes on each other, but this is beyond boundaries!"

"I wouldn't joke about this. I'm not that cruel. I need for you to come and identify her body."

Eric gave him the card to the medical examiner's office and left. Once in his car he looked back to see Mr. Peterson looking down at the card while Mrs. Peterson ran back in the house. He hated being the bearer of bad news. He went back to the precinct to hear an update on the last girl. All he needed was to have to go back out to tell another parent that their daughter was dead. He was met by the captain. He signaled for him to come into his office.

"How you doin' Eric?"

"I hate this aspect of the job. Just would rather delivered a baby than this."

"Understandable. Here's a glimmer of light. The last girl is still alive."

"What? The one mangled in the backseat of the car? You're kidding! When I was talking to the firefighters they were all baffled to how she even survived it. She was literally crushed in between the back seat and the braking system of the rear of the car. They all said that she should have been mangled to death."

"Weird isn't it?"

"Yeah. At least I don't have to tell her parents she's dead yet."

Eric walked back out to punch out for the day. He couldn't help remembering, or trying to remember about an old saying that his grandmother used to say about this sort of thing happening. Something about the Lord's will and angels. He needed something to get over seeing all that death and dismay. Seeing the accident made him appreciate the fact that his daughter was still little. Meagan was only 5, and now seeing this accident made him want to keep her small forever. He knew all of the girls, their peers called them the 3A's, because you never saw one without one of the others around. They were all smart, and looking forward to going to college in the fall. All changed by taking a drink.

He went into his house, and his wife knew that the day was already going bad for him. She came up to him and hugged him. She wanted to say to him that it was time for him to find something else, that he didn't have to follow in his dad's footsteps. She wanted him to smile again like he did before he thought about police academy, when he worked in the factory. She enjoyed making lunches for him and teasing him about the smell of his clothes. She didn't have to worry about him being shot at, let alone having to chase after anyone or even this, tell a parent that their kid was gone.

He hugged her back, and for the first time in years he cried. The longer he cried the tighter she held him. She didn't try to stop the tears—they were well deserved, and he deserved to let them free. She had cried hers when she heard about the accident on the local news. She only imagined how the parents of the deceased girls must be taking it. Once he stopped crying she offered him some juice, and asked if he was hungry. He wasn't, but took the juice. She sat at the table with him. Tonight was supposed to be their date night. He was going to have to pull himself together. She broke his train of thought.

"Honey, we don't have to go out tonight. We can go and get Meagan and just have pizza if you like."

"No, I don't want to disappoint you. We've hadn't had one in months."

"I won't be disappointed. Just glad you're home safe. How bad was it?"

"Very. Two dead. One alive, but they rushed her to the trauma center. Ugliest scene I've ever seen. They all should be dead, especially the one that was in the back seat. She's the one that is still alive."

"What? I thought that the girl that was on the passenger side was still alive?"

"No. The one in the back seat is still alive. The driver we found about 25 feet up. She was thrown from the car and then hit by a semi. The front seat passenger was damn near decapitated and just bled out. They were about to put the car on a flatbed when they saw the arm of the last girl. She was caught between the braking system and the back seat. The car was no bigger than a Volkswagen when whatever hit it was through."

"Wow! Her parents...."

"They're at the hospital I assume. They didn't give me that detail. The officers that were on duty a couple of them lost their lunch at the sight of how the girls looked. Think one of the guys fainted."

"Fainted?"

"Fainted."

"Enough talk about it. I want to forget it. I want to go out on the town with my favorite girl."

"You sure? We can eat pizza and catch some football."

"Positive. I'm going to get all handsome, and you're going to get all pretty, and we're going out. You know, celebrate life."

His wife went off to get herself dressed for their date. He went into the bathroom to shower. As the water ran over him he hoped that a night out would help him shake off what he had saw earlier in the day. He was just thankful that it wasn't someone he loved in that situation. The 3A's—Anastasia, Alexandra and Angelica. He remembered that Alex had the biggest crush on him. It was so bad that she would get in trouble just to see him come out in his police car when he was a rookie. Even though he was 6 years older than her she never stopped trying to get his attention between boyfriends.

Now she was gone. She had just turned 19 a couple of days before the accident. He knew her parents were going to be devastated.

"How is she today, doc?" the nurse said.

"Same. Just don't understand it. Are they sure she was in the back of the car?"

"Why you say that? They said they found her only when they were about to put the car on the flatbed to take it away."

"Was she conscious? How did they find her?"

"You'll have to ask the officers that. Why all the concern?"

"Well, she's healing faster than expected."

"Faster? I don't understand."

"Neither do I."

Angelica heard them talking. She wanted to reach out to them, to let them know that she was there and listening. But her body felt like lead, and she hurt all over. Her mouth felt like a combination of sandpaper and paste. She wondered how long had she been there. Had Alex and Stasi come to see her? She wished for the strength to be able to let them know that she was listening. The only thing that kept her calm was someone humming songs. They sounded like church songs, but she would sleep every time she would hear one. Then came the light. Bright light.

She looked up sheltering her eyes. *Wait, I can move my arms? I must be dead!! I can see. Yep, I'm dead. My mom's going to lose his mind. Where am I? I don't see any pearly gates. Where am I?*

The hand on her shoulder startled her. She turned around to see an older lady smiling at her. "You're not in heaven, at least not yet."

"I don't......oh boy.....I'm in hell?"

The lady smiled at her. "No, you're in limbo. Guess God's got plans for you."

"What? God? I don't understand!!"

"What do you remember?"

As hard as she tried Angelica couldn't remember anything. She didn't even know what day of the week it was. She began to cry. "I can't remember!"

"It'll come back to you. You have work to do."

"I don't understand! You're saying that I'm not in heaven, not in hell, but in limbo. Then I can't remember anything! What day is it?"

"Wednesday."

"Wednesday? I've been sleeping for 6 days? I'm going to be fired from my job! My mother's going to kill me!!"

"You really don't remember do you? Come with me."

Angelica followed the lady. "Look down."

She looked down as the lady instructed. There she saw herself in the hospital bed, bruised up like she got jumped by a whole gang of men. "Why am I just lying there, I'm talking to you! Where are you at in the room? That room isn't bright at all. What's going on?'

"It's time for you to remember, and to live." As fast as she said that Angelica was back in her body and sitting up in her hospital bed. The world as she would know it change, and change for the better. As she sat in the hospital bed with all the alarms going off the nurse rushed in to see what the matter was. The first nurse in dropped her tablet when she saw her sitting up. "Doctor! Doctor!" she screamed as she ran out of the room. Her screams became fainter as she got farther away. The aide came in and stood in the doorway frozen, "My God!" What was she, some type of monster?

The doctor came back in with the nurse in tow. "Well, Miss Carroll, you are a survivor!!" Angelica made the sign for to write. She wrote, "What day is it? Where are my friends?"

The doctor hung his head. He looked at her not wanting to tell her about her friends. "How do you feel? You're pretty banged up."

"WHAT DAY IS IT? WHERE IS MY MOTHER? WHERE ARE MY FRIENDS?!!!"

"First things first. I don't need you upset. You've been through a lot. Today is November 18, 2001. You've been here for over a month."

"What? Where are my friends? Does my mother know I'm here?"

"Your mother knows that you're here. You just missed her dropping through. It's been a hard month for her."

"And my friends?"

"What do you remember before this?"

"Doc, please where are my friends?!!"

"They're gone."

"Gone home. Thank God. What happened?"

Before he could answer her mother came in tears to see her. He was glad of the reprieve. He used it to exit. Leave it to her mother to tell her that she was the only survivor of the accident. He didn't have the heart to. Every day he would look at her when she was in her coma he valued his daughters all the more. He wouldn't know what he would have done if he'd lost his daughter like that. By all medical reasoning she should have been dead. Yet here she was alive, only being found that way through the grace of God himself. What would have happened if her arm didn't fall out when it did? She'd been buried in the car, mashed up when the car would have been scrapped out and crushed.

Her mother kissed her face. She was so glad to see her pull through. The month has been hard—the Petersons and Weber's had buried their daughters, and they inwardly hated that her daughter was still alive. Mrs. Webster even went to her and told her that she was waiting for her daughter to die for she could feel the pain that she was feeling. She thought that the remark was hateful, seeing that she didn't know whether or not Angelica was going to survive or not. After the funeral she stayed to herself, looking at pictures of her daughter through the years. She would hope that the next day Angelica would be knocking on the door, or sitting at the table eating her usual junk food for breakfast.

However day in and day out she was in the house alone with her daughter in the hospital. All her mother could do was pray that God would do his will in her daughter's life. If only she knew what she was really praying for her daughter's life. She fell back on her old ancestry. She had another visit from the woman that had visited her at her home years before. She smiled at her. "What are you smiling about?"

"She is the one. It's been a long while since there's been one here."

"My daughter is what? Who are you really? You're not who you said you were. That woman died decades ago!"

She woman smiled. "From the outside, you're talking to yourself.

You didn't settle here by accident. You were brought here—you both were. Your daughter will be far stronger than you though."

"What are you talking about? My daughter is here in the hospital!"

"And her body is healing by the day. Part of her inner strength. While your prayers helped keep her from falling total prey to the evil influences in this town, your strength enough is not enough to do what needs to be done."

"And who are you to say what I am or what my daughter is? Why don't you go away!"

"As you wish. My dealings are done with you. I will come to your daughter in time. The books are hers."

"You will not come near her! My God will bring her through! Away shaman!"

Her faith gotten her through the tough times that she experienced here with Fannie Gray and her evil. Now she was awake after a month. She didn't care how she looked after the accident, she would still see her as her beautiful daughter. As she went up to her she couldn't help but smile. Angelica was wondering what all was going on.

Her mother hugged her so tight that she cried out in pain. "I'm so sorry!! I've missed you! Didn't know whether you were going to live or die! But I knew that God had you in his hand!!"

She didn't understand what was her mother was talking about, or what all the excitement was about. To her she was the last one going home from the hospital, and her friends would probably tease her for taking so long. After her mother hugged her she asked her the question about her friends. Her mother dropped her head. "Baby, they're dead. Alex just got buried three weeks ago."

She looked at her mother in disbelief. What did she mean that they were dead? What had happened? Why couldn't she remember? Her mother reached out to hold her again when she pulled away. She wanted her to leave. She wanted to be alone. Whoever thought that this joke was funny it stopped being that way when it included her friends. Her mother gave her the space she needed. She was just glad that she was awake. The doctors marveled at how she had healed. She came in broken—ribs, legs, arms, collar bone, ankles, and pelvis.

And now in a month's time her collar bone was healed, and so were most of her ribs. They didn't even understand how she could sit up on a broken pelvis and her spine which had been broken in several places. The doctors didn't understand, but her mother did. It was the shaman.

Angelica couldn't believe that her friends were dead. What happened to them? Her answers would come when Eric Daily came to question her later that day.

"Hello Angelica. I have some questions to ask you."

Angelica couldn't write fast enough to ask her questions. "Is it true that Alex and Stasia are dead? Tell me this is some cruel joke!"

"They are. Do you remember anything?"

"No. What happened?"

He showed her the pictures of the car. She recoiled. He watched the expression on her face as she took a look at the picture. "Was I in here?"

They were interrupted by the doctor who motioned for Eric to come out of the room. "She won't remember anything for a while."

"Is that an effect from the accident?"

"It is. I'm waiting for her mother to come back. Some other things turned up."

"Thanks." Eric went back in to see her still looking at the picture. "Don't stress yourself about the picture. I'm going to try and help you, ok?"

"Okay."

"Can you remember what you did on the 15th of October?"

She thought back. "An invite to a party. Todd was giving it for all the grads. Stasi was excited about getting invited. She had the biggest crush on Todd. My mom didn't want me to go to the party, we argued about it that day."

Eric was glad that there was some of her memory intact, but decided to go slow. "Did your mom know that you went to the party?"

"We argued till the day of. Wished I'd listened to her. Something bad must have happened to me to get me here. Something bad involving that car. Was I driving?"

"No, you weren't. Alex was."

"Oh." The tears began to flow. Eric stopped the questions for the day, but left the pictures. Maybe she was holding back what she knew. As he left he overheard a bit of the conversation between the doctor and her mother. Something about a clot on Angelica's brain. That didn't sound good to him, he just hoped that he would get some type of answers before she too would pass away.

"No, I'm not signing that paper for you to cut on her again! She's been through enough! God will heal her!! He's doing it already!"

"You don't understand Mrs. Carroll, if we don't she's going to hemorrhage to death."

"Has she so far? The answer is still no." She turned and went into her daughter's room. To Mrs. Carroll the doctors did all that they could do. The rest was on God. She looked at her daughter lying down and came to her. She didn't say anything, but noticed the picture of the accident on her nightstand. She motioned to throw it away when she stopped her. "I want to remember. I need to remember."

Her mother frowned, wanting her to concentrate more on getting well than something from her past. "The doctors want to operate on you again, I told them no."

"Why? What did they want to operate on?"

"Your brain. I said no. Too dangerous, I might lose you for good."

"You will eventually anyway."

"Don't talk like that!!"

"We all must die. How else are we to meet with our heavenly father?"

Her mother stood there shocked. Angelica never said anything on a religious context since she stopped going to church. Her mother was speechless.

"We know not the day or the hour of when God is going to call us home, so we must persevere, running the race of faith. Believing that he loves us and wants us with him."

For a minute or two there was silence in the room. Then it happened. Angelica got up and walked. Her mother fainted.

Hours later Angelica would find herself on the x-ray table. The doctors were more baffled than ever. Her pelvis and spine was healed. Injuries like hers should have left her with little mobility at all. In fact, they were about to tell her mother that they were going to send her home in a wheelchair before the x-ray. Her mother smiled, God was working a miracle in her daughter. It was he who sent the shaman to her. She didn't know all what she did, but she thanked God for sending her through. She even was seeing it with what she was saying. What her mother didn't understand was what she was seeing in her daughter was only the beginning.

Four days later the hospital released Angelica. The Petersons and Weber's heard the news and made it a point to come over to the Carroll's home. Marlon Peterson arrived first with his wife in tow. Known to be a hell raiser, Marlon Peterson was going to speak his mind no matter whose feelings got hurt. Angelica's mother saw the couple as they got out of the car. She made sure the door was locked and went to Angelica's bedroom. "The Petersons are at the door. Don't answer it."

Having her energy back Angelica asked, "Why? They are coming to see me. No need to fear or hide from them or anyone else anymore."

"Angelica they're angry. They want you dead just like their daughters. Please go to your room for your safety."

"I want to hear what they want to know. I'm not afraid."

Her mother had enough of the insults from the people of the town that listened to both the Weber's and Petersons. She stayed to herself, just enduring at work and coming home. Angelica met Mr. Peterson at the door. He looked her up and down as he pushed his way through the door. "I guess you're happy now! You managed to survive while my daughter died! Were you even in the car?"

"The officers on the scene said that I was. I don't remember much about the accident."

"Bullshit! Why did you let my daughter drive drunk! It's your fault she's dead!"

"He that's without sin cast the first stone. You came here in anger, but really you're hurt and angry at your loss."

"Save that religious bullshit for the church! You killed her!"

"Mr. Peterson, I wasn't driving. They said that they found me in the back seat. If I was driving wouldn't I be dead?"

"You should be! You killed my daughter you bitch! You're the blame for her being gone!"

Mrs. Peterson stepped in. "How did you survive? Why you?"

"I don't know Mr. and Mrs. Peterson, and I'm having a hard time adjusting to the fact that my best friends are gone while I'm still here. I've been trying to remember to the day of the accident, but can only remember what happened a few days before."

"Best friends my ass! My wife may be simple to believe you, but I don't believe anything you've said! You were jealous of Alex because she was prettier than you!"

Mrs. Peterson's stance softened, however, Mr. Peterson's didn't. His anger continued to boil. Not only had he lost his daughter, he had lost Anastasia, the young woman that he truly loved. He was planning to divorce his wife and marry her. His wife no longer did anything for him, and they only stayed together because of their status in the community. He stepped forward with his hand in his pocket. Angelica stood there watching him. "Since you continue to be self-seeking and reject the truth to entertain evil, you will continue to seek revenge and be angry. So please forgive me for any wrong I have done to you."

"I don't forgive you! You need to die like my daughter did!" Mr. Peterson pulled out the revolver and fired a shot. Everything went into slow motion to Angelica. A crash of dishes. Two screams. Another shot. A thump. Two screams. Her mother on the phone. Her moving. Then as fast as things went slow they came back into focus. She stood there in front of Mr. Peterson, his wife was on the floor bleeding. Her mother called the police and ambulance. Where was the other bullet? Where did it go? She was certain she heard another shot. The shots scared away the Weber's from coming up the front.

Marlon Peterson stood there with anger in his eyes. "See what you've done! You'll burn in hell, even if I have to put you there!!"

He aimed to fire again. The policeman tased him before he could make the shot and apprehended him. His wife lay on the floor bleeding profusely. "I told him it wasn't your fault…..you're………... shot too………….."

She didn't feel the bullet go in. She was more concerned about Mrs. Peterson's health. She held on to her hand as they both were loaded into the ambulance. While on the ride Mrs. Peterson was trying to talk to her. She looked down at her "Not going……….. forgive you……….see Alex………" She felt her hand going slack. The medic dove in to try to get her heart going again. Angelica sat there. *Lord, no more loss. Not like this. Not like this.*

The woman she saw while she was in the hospital was back again. "Why not her? She wanted to go, and it was her time."

"She had so much going for her."

"She lost the desire to live after her daughter died. She gave up everything, so why not her life?"

"That's heartless to say!"

"Not really, she caught a bullet for you. The first one would have killed you instantly."

"And that would have been fine with me."

"That's not how it works. Why don't you let her die? Everything dies at some point or another."

"Who are you? How can you say who dies and who lives?"

"That is my calling. It will be yours soon. Embrace it. It's coming"

The lady disappeared as fast as she appeared. Didn't these guys see her? They kept on talking as though they didn't see her at all.

"Marc, turn off the siren, she's gone. This other one will be ok." He covered her head over. Angelica went up to him and asked why he covered her. "She's dead. We cover their faces."

"She's just sleep. She's still breathing."

"Sit back, she's not breathing she's dead."

"Ye of little faith. She is just sleeping." She moved toward her. The medic went on to what he was doing. She was dead, and the girl left on his ambulance was nuts. Angelica placed her hand on her chest and looked at her. She said to herself, *Lord, this woman has so much to live for. Don't take her now. I need her to help me remember. Give her some more time.* Mrs. Peterson sat straight up and gasped, scaring the hell out of the medic in the back. "Holy shit! What did you do to her?" Angelica sat back in her seat waiting for the ride to end.

At the hospital they rushed Mrs. Peterson into surgery, while some nurses tended to Angelica's wounds. One of the nurses came out to the medic. "I thought you said that she got shot in the shoulder?"

"She was bleeding from her shoulder." The nurse gave him a bullet. "She gave this to me. What is going on?"

"I don't know, but it's freaky. The woman that you rushed to surgery died about 15 minutes ago. She touched her and she started back breathing."

The nurse went back into where Angelica was. She had left. Where had she gone?

Angelica didn't feel hurt. She felt that hospitals were for those that were truly injured. She walked out of the emergency room and out toward the front of the hospital. She stopped at the chapel. She sat inside, and embraced the quiet. She thought to herself, *I didn't kill anyone, so why am I to blame?"*

The voice came to her along with a dim light. *It's easier for some to blame others rather than take responsibility. It was not your fault the accident occurred. God doesn't make mistakes. You were spared to do his work.*

*What work am I to do? I'm not into that God thing.*

*He's into you. He will work through you. There are people that he needs to get his message to. He will direct you to them.* The light disappeared and she was left with the quietness of the chapel.

She looked at the figure of Jesus on the cross. *I feel like you. On display. Wounded. No one helping me down, just watching.*

The priest walked toward her. "Odd to find someone in here. Was about to close it up for the day. You seem puzzled. Can I help?"

"I don't think so. Just looking at the statue of Jesus on the cross. There he hangs for all to see, wounded and in pain, with no one to get him down."

"Jesus and the cross wasn't about him getting down. It was about sacrifice. He came to earth to give us a chance at heaven."

"So many people don't have time for that. They don't feed into all the Jesus stuff."

"And you? What do you think?"

"I think that he sacrificed all for nothing. Man still is as cutthroat as ever."

"Not all. Jesus came for everyone, even those that refuse to accept his gift. We still have free will. He never forced his beliefs on anyone. He led by example."

"Yeah, I heard all the stories. The two fish and five loaves of bread, the story of the dead man being raised from the dead. That's all they are, stories."

"Why don't you believe there's any truth to them?"

"Because God doesn't really care about everybody, only those that put time and effort into him. He's like a business. No money or time in, no rewards out."

"He's not like that at all. That's how man wants him to be. Since you say he's like a business let me put his importance in a way you can understand. There's billions of people on the planet, right?"

"Right."

"Then he thinks enough of billions of people to wake them up every day."

"And the ones that don't?"

"He only promised man threescore and ten."

"What is that?"

"Seventy years."

"Some people don't live that long. And the babies. His business is himself. He only cares about those that commit to his laws."

"You are so wrong. Just try him out. You sound much like Thomas in the bible."

"Thomas?"

"Yes. He was a disciple of Jesus that when Jesus came back from the dead he refused to believe what others said they had seen."

"Don't blame him there."

"Then Jesus came to him and he told Jesus to his face that he wouldn't believe he raised from the dead unless he saw all his marks. Jesus showed him his hands and his stomach. The wounds were there and Thomas touched them. You've heard of the phrase, 'doubting Thomas' that's where that comes from."

"And when he did all of that what happened?"

"Take a bible and read the book of Matthew. When you leave out the door will lock behind you." The priest took his leave. She took a bible and went to the book of Matthew. She read the book. She felt so sorry for how Jesus' life ended on earth. Falsely accused, lied on, abandoned by his people, Peter being a coward, beaten in public, treated like dirt. When it came time for him to be crucified on the cross not one of his disciples came to offer to carry his cross for him. She related to Jesus' plight. She took the bible and left out of the chapel. She walked right into her mother. "Girl, where have you been? The nurses have been looking all over for you!!"

"Mom, I'm all right. How is Mrs. Peterson?"

"I don't know or care!"

"You should. I wouldn't want anyone dying in my doorway. Is she OK? They rushed her out so fast."

"My concern is you. I can care less about the Petersons or the Weber's or any of these people that live here!"

"Why? What have they done to you?"

"Just open your eyes girl! Mr. Peterson just tried to kill you! Has it sunk in?"

It did. She looked at her mother. Her mother looked at her puzzled. She was holding a bible. For years she had begged and pleaded for her to go to church with her, or at least read her bible that had collected dust long ago. They walked out to the car. She asked her mother the question again. "Is Mrs. Peterson ok? Did she die?"

"NO! Be concerned about yourself!! These people don't care about you! They want you and me dead!"

"Why! Why do they want me dead? What has happened to turn them against me?"

"You remember! You have to!"

"I don't. Remember the days before. How you didn't want me to go to the party. I've been told that I was in a car accident. I know that Stasi and Alex are dead. Just pieces."

Her mother looked at her. She didn't remember. Her defenses lowered. "Sorry baby, it's been rough since the accident. People haven't been friendly. They found you in the back seat by the brake system of the car. Alex had been thrown from the car."

"She was driving? So that means that Stasi was on the passenger side."

"Yes. Her head was damn near cut clear off her body. They both died on site. They only found you when the lifted the car up to take it away and your arm fell. You're the only survivor of the accident."

Angelica sat in the car sorrowful. She should have died right along with her girlfriends. But why was she spared? What was so special that she should live? Her mother answered her question for her.

"Angel, you were blessed all along!"

"I don't understand."

"I pray for you all the time even when we fight. This town is wicked! God with his angels ensured your safety!! He has something for you to do!"

She didn't understand all her mother's excitement about it all. What did God have for her to do? Who was this strange lady that was popping up talking to her that no one else saw? It was going to be a long night. Maybe some answers would present themselves soon. The rest of the ride was long and quiet, her mother humming her favorite gospel tune. She looked down at the bible, maybe it had answers for her. They arrived home to Mrs. Weber sitting on their porch. Her mother took defense mode. "What do you want now? Haven't you all targeted my home enough? All you church folk!"

"I just want to know what the last thing Anastasia said was. How she looked. Did she suffer long?"

Her mother was about to shoot her away when Angelica looked at her. Her mother stormed past Mrs. Weber into the house. In her mind none of them deserved answers to anything.

"Mrs. Weber, all I remember are bits and pieces. It was a nice party. Alcohol was served. We all drank, me not so much. Stasi knew that she was too drunk to drive. Alex wanted me to, I wanted to take a cab and leave the car."

Mrs. Weber held her head down. "She could have called us. Her dad would have fussed, but at least…..at least…" Mrs. Weber broke down in tears.

Angelica sat next to her. "I wished that I died too. I don't belong here."

Mrs. Weber looked at Angelica. "Embrace life. You were spared for a reason. Hopefully it would come to you what it is." Mrs. Weber got up and dusted herself off. "I miss my baby so much."

"I miss her too. Feels odd without them clowning around." She turned around to see her mother glaring at Mrs. Weber. "Are you alright mother?"

"I will be when this woman gets off of my porch. She acts all remorseful now but wasn't like that a week ago! Get out of here!! Tell your hateful friends that they need to stop ruining my home because of what happened! You all should have done this to Fannie Gray!!"

Mrs. Weber was shocked to hear that name. Fannie Gray. She remembered how she treated people in the village. Mrs. Weber went on to her car and drove off. The tension was still so thick that Angelica decided to go to her room and keep her distance from her mother. At one point in time both Mrs. Weber and Peterson were good friends with her mother. Now her mother hated them all. She wasn't the mother that she had grown up with, she was a bitter woman. Her heart went out to her friend's parents. The loss was too great. And for her to be standing there alive was harder still. She drifted into sleep when the light woke her. It was so bright that she shielded her eyes from it. She heard a familiar voice. It was her grandmother's. It couldn't be, her grandmother had been dead for over 10 years. But she knew that it was her without a doubt.

"Hello dear."

"Grandma? I can't see you!"

"You don't need to. Listen to what I have to say. Keep your mind focused. You have the mission to destroy the evil here."

"How can I do that?"

"One thing at a time. Start at the accident. You have to open your mind and heart."

"Grandma, why am I still here? I should be dead. Why?"

"Only the good Lord knows that. You'll have to ask him that. But you have work to do. Heal the hearts that you can. But it's time for the evil to be out of this place."

As fast as she said those few words she was gone. How was she to heal people here? It wasn't her fault that she survived. She didn't look forward to this 'task' she was here for. She laid back down to try and rest. Tomorrow would be another day.

Her mother lay in her bed staring at the wall. She was happy that her daughter was here with her. She was saddened by the other girls dying, but it was time for all the others to get over it and let her and her daughter live their lives. She was tired of the hatred, and didn't want her daughter exposed to it. It blew her mind that Marlon Peterson would go to the extent to try and kill her. What was next? He reminded her so much of Fannie Gray. She fell asleep feeling like she had opened up Pandora's Box.

The next day Angelica had her own agenda. She wanted to see for herself was Mrs. Peterson alright. As she walked to the bus stop she noticed the pointing of fingers and whispering. As the bus slowed down people shifted around as if she had the plague. She paid them no mind, and sat comfortably until her destination. Once she got off everyone moved around on the bus was relieved. As she entered the hospital to the reception area she couldn't help but feel that someone was watching her. She turned around to see Eric Daily.

"Funny to see you here. I was just coming to see Mrs. Peterson."

"How is she?"

"I don't know. What happened at your house?"

"They came to talk to me. Mr. Peterson was angry with me and blamed me for his daughter's death. I told him that I wasn't driving, so how could I have done anything. While I was talking to him he got angrier and angrier. His wife seen the gun before I did and jumped in front of him. She got the worst of it. I feel so bad. Worse than when the accident occurred."

"What did he say after the gun went off? Did he realize that he shot his wife?"

"I don't think it clicked. All he wanted was for me to die. Said that I didn't deserve to be here if his daughter wasn't. He would have emptied out his gun if the police hadn't tased him."

"Wasn't you afraid of him killing you?"

"I'm already dead. Think about it. I'm just out of place."

Those words chilled Eric to the bone. Already dead? Out of place? They got into the elevator together up to Mrs. Peterson's room. She got out of the elevator and was stopped by all the commotion going on the floor. As they made their way closer to Mrs. Peterson's room they saw what the ruckus was about. Mr. Peterson was being carted out by officers. Eric went up to his fellow officers wanting to know what happened.

"What's going on? Why is he here?"

"Got permission to see his wife. He didn't believe that he shot his wife. He lost it when he saw her hooked up."

"Is she alright?"

"Yeah, she's alright. The prosecution is going for attempted murder."

"They'll get it."

While Eric was talking to his fellow officers Angelica walked into the room. Mrs. Peterson was glad to see her. She walked over to her bedside and held her hand. She looked up to her smiling. "I'm tired. I want to see my baby."

Angelica returned the smile. "She would want you to help your husband get through this. You leave he'll lose it."

"He shot me. He saw me come between you and him. He didn't care. Hasn't in a long while. He thinks I don't know that he doesn't love me."

"Anger is a very strong emotion. It makes us do things we normally won't do if it goes on unchecked. Be angry, but don't sin.

He is your husband, pray for him. He's so angry that I survived. I'm angry too."

"But you're not going around shooting people!" she said as she began to cough. "I saw her yesterday."

"Saw who?"

"Alex. She was just as beautiful as the day she was born. She was telling me to just let go and come with her."

"That wasn't your daughter. Tricks of the devil. He wants your soul."

Mrs. Peterson looked at her. "It was her." She turned away from Angelica. Eric entered the room. Somehow he knew that he had missed his opportunity to talk to Mrs. Peterson. He looked at her. "You should have stayed at home. You weren't needed here. Haven't you caused enough pain?"

She began to understand now what her mother was going though, and what made her so bitter toward the townspeople. Hate. Pain. Sorrow. She walked out of the hospital. She sat in the front at the bus stop when a little girl came up to her pointing behind her smiling. "You have a broken circle on your head!"

She felt on top of her head for a circle. Nothing. There was no mirror for her to see what was on her head. The little girl kept pointing at her until her mother corrected her. She looked at her in shock. "What are you?"

"A young woman. What do you mean what am I?"

"You're not human! You can't be!" the woman scooped up her daughter and ran.

*Now what? Bad enough that the whole town hates me. Now I have a broken circle and scaring off innocent people. What could go wrong next?*

She decided to walk home instead of waiting on the bus. She had a lot of things on her mind, and the walk would do her good. She had started on her way when she began to sing. She was singing gospel songs that she only heard once or twice as a child. As she sung more the better she felt. She sat down midway to her home resting for a bit to enjoy the day. Her thoughts were interrupted by an old lady.

"Hello, dear. How are you?"

"Fine, and yourself? Didn't hear you come up, must been caught up in my thoughts."

"That's fine. You need to hide your halo."

"My what?" She gave her a mirror. She looked in horror at what she was seeing. "What in the world is happening?"

"Hard to explain. But you've been given a chance to do something here. You know what it is already."

"Can everybody see this halo?"

"No. Just those that believe. Just like you."

"In God?"

"Yes! You called out to him before the crash. You prayed that you would get home safely."

"But I didn't. We didn't. My friends were killed and I was caught mangled in the car."

"They never believed. Never was instilled in them. But you're different. Raised different. Let's walk. Don't want people to think that you're crazy."

"What do you mean?"

"You're the only one that can see me. Walk on, it'll seem like your singing."

"Why am I here? I can't do anything here. So much hate and bitterness. I didn't call the shots on what happened. I wasn't even driving! What do they want? Why so much hatred towards my mother?"

"You know what you would want if that was you. Help them."

She kept on walking after the lady had left. There was so much hurt left behind because of the accident. So much bitterness. What would her friends do if it was one of them? She would start small. She went straight into her room. Her mother hadn't made it in, and that was good. She had become more angry and bitter, and stopped going to church since she had come home. She looked up to her mother as a rock after her dad had disappeared from the scene. To see her like this was not good. She had let the ill tide of the accident take away her joy.

Since the accident Angelica had more spiritual visitors than she did friends. They all were telling her the same thing—save who you can and get rid of the evil in this town. Who did they think she was, God? But she knew it was something strange about this town, how there wasn't a lot of children here. She dismissed it as the town being more suited for older people and those raising their last children to send them off for college. If only she really knew. She eventually fell asleep wondering what would happen next.

Grace peeped in on Angelica, her angel. She didn't know how she survived the crash, didn't want to know how. As she looked at her sleeping she looked strange to her. What was that glow around her? What was she seeing? She wanted to wake her up, but dismissed it. Maybe it was the lighting from behind her or she was just seeing things. She closed her door, leaving it slightly ajar and went to her room. She had a long day, and she wanted to get off her feet. She couldn't understand how the bullet that Marlon Peterson fired at her from close range didn't kill her.

Angelica felt the hand on her leg and woke out of her sleep. She knew that touch, and wiped her eyes as she looked around. No white lights, no grandma, just her sitting on a rock in a clearing in a forest. What was she doing here? She knew better than to call out, she walked around to see if anything would be familiar—nothing. Then that's when she saw her. She looked strange from a distance. It was Alex her friend, or someone that looked an awful lot like her. She didn't proceed to her, but looked in her direction. Alex broke the silence.

"So now you don't know me? You can't speak?"

This personification of what was supposed to be her friend was mean and nasty. She tried to speak, but found her mouth and throat dry as a board. Alex spoke again.

"You should be here with me, dead. You let me drive drunk! You are the reason that both Stasi and I are here!"

She still fought for the voice to speak but couldn't. She wanted to move closer to her for a look to see if her eyes were playing tricks on her and she found that she couldn't do that either, as if they were separated by an invisible wall. Alex continued on with her nasty remarks. "You partied with us, you drank with us, and you did what we did. How did you live and we get put here? I want to live like you! I hate this place! No rest at all!"

She still tried to talk but gave up on trying. She couldn't explain to her how she survived because she didn't fully understand it. She wondered where Stasi was. It wouldn't be long until she found her answer. She moved away from where Alex had been standing with her shouting and cursing at her to another part of the forest. There she saw Stasi crying. For a moment she felt sorry for her, until Stasi caught sight of her. She stood up and looked at her. "Why didn't you save me? Why couldn't you drive that night? We would have all lived if you've drove."

This time she found that she was able to speak. "Stasi, I tried to talk Alex into taking a cab, remember. I was in no shape to drive either."

"You was the most sober of us all! You caused me to be here!"

"Where is here?"

"Hell."

"Stasi, I thought that you went to church?"

"What does that have to do with me being here? It's your fault I'm dead in the first place! And you the most sinful of all of us gets to live! It's bullshit! Your head should have been cut off like mine was. My mother fainted when she saw me!"

"It's not my fault for the accident or the choice you made to get you here. I don't even know how I survived. But I thought you believed in God."

"I went to church because I had to. I didn't pay attention to all that mumbo jumbo they were talking about. Every now and then I'd make out in parts of the basement with my boyfriend. Or even find a new one there. You never even stepped foot in a church, and you're alive. Why? How?"

"I don't know. I know that I should be dead. Like you."

"The last thing I remember was arguing with my mother about what I was wearing. I wanted to look good for my boyfriend. All gone…..it happened so quick. What was she doing to cause the crash?"

"I don't know. I don't. The car was totaled where I was at. Alex was thrown from the car then hit again trying to get up I was told. You were…."

"Head was almost off my body"

She stood there and looked at her. She began to fade away. "So many things I would have done different if I had a second chance. All gone. My poor parents!"

Angelica looked as she faded away. She began to think *'why was she brought out here in the middle of nowhere? And why are dead people having a conversation with me?* She tried to go back to sleep, but found herself tossing and turning. Finally she got up and went downstairs. Her mother was downstairs drinking tea.

"What are you doing up?"

"Couldn't sleep. Bad dreams."

"About what? The accident?"

"No, just my girlfriends blaming me for living while they're dead. I don't understand it."

"Don't lose sleep over them. Just the way the restless dead communicate."

"One of my friends says she's in hell. How do you go back to sleep after hearing that?"

"You can. You'll learn how to. That won't be the last dream you'll have about them. So much hurt and pain. It'll come to you what you need to do. The girls are just telling you in spirit what they felt about you all along. It'll get worse before it gets better."

"What are they going to do?"

"If you let them, cause you many sleepless nights. They now know that they made poor choices in life."

"So did I!"

"Not like them. I never really cared for Alexandra. She was very promiscuous and wanted you to be that way. Anastasia just wanted to belong like you did, and Alexandra was the "it" girl. Whatever the boys wanted she was "it". Anastasia measured both of you up, and I believe that she was trying to be like you."

"What? A young woman that's scared of her own shadow? You don't understand how it feels?"

"To not be having your legs open and call it love? That's not love, that's lust. And the only thing you get out of it if you're not careful are diseases and babies. Yeah girls tease you, but at least your name isn't on the health department roster for having a STD. I guess a little church stuck in you."

"I just want for the dreams to stop. I don't know why I'm here. There's nothing I can do for anyone."

"Really? God seems to think otherwise."

"I just wish He could tell me what it is he wants me to do! All this hatred about an accident!"

"Drink this tea, calm your nerves. The hatred was there before the accident. There's a lot going on in this town—an evil force that consumes it. It's hidden behind the people here. Neither of their parents liked me because I go to church so much. I like to do things with the church, and I don't have time for games and keeping up. As you were told, there is a hell, and I'm not trying to be there the rest of my eternal life. I think you're getting a chance to do the same."

Angelica sat there at the table feeling woozy. She had become very tired. She finished her tea and went back into her bedroom. She laid on the pillows, and within minutes was sound asleep. The tea her mother gave her would help her rest as it did for her so many nights. Her mother knew that she would have to cherish each moment with her daughter before the good Lord would take her away. She was amazed at how she was embracing her mission. Who knows, maybe the good Lord would take them both from this sinful world. But first she was being tested to see what she could do for this evil town they lived in. Fannie although dead still had an influence in this town.

Olive Weber went to see her daughter's grave. The least violent of all the parents Angelica was moved to start there. She brought flowers to her gravesite. The rustle of leaves caused Mrs. Weber to turn around.

"I didn't mean to disturb you."

"Just wanted to be near her. I miss her so much."

"So do I. Feels weird her not being around talking about what she's going to do with her hair."

"Yes! That girl and all her hair colors! I remember one time she tried to dye it red and it turned out orange!" Angelica remembered her cutting it into a mohawk and adding colors to it for Halloween.

"Whose idea was it for her to do the Mohawk?" she asked.

"Girl, I don't know! But the look on her dad's face the next day was priceless. Anytime she had to go into public with him she had to wear a scarf or a hat! I thought that he was going to have a heart attack when he saw what she did!" They laughed together. Then they looked at the grave. "What do you…"

"I remember Stasi driving to the party. We knew that we were going to make an entrance. Alex would always say that we needed a theme song. I was just glad to get out of the house and out of going to church with my mom."

"Maybe that's where my baby should have been. I think that her being friends with Alex was the worst decision she made."

"Why?"

"You know how Alex was. All into boys and sex, drinking smoking, anything that could get her to stay in the limelight. A lot of the grown men had slept with her, and I questioned whether or not my husband knew about it or not. Stasia thought that she was the person to be. You were different. While you liked the popularity, you didn't go all out like Stasia to be something you wasn't."

"We all did our share of mischief."

"I know. It broke her dad's heart when he found out that his little girl wasn't a virgin anymore. How did your mother take it?"

"I was grounded for a month. But she also took me to the doctor to get me on birth control. I guess she didn't want me to make the same mistakes she did. I didn't sleep with anybody. Too afraid to with those guys Alex kept up with."

"Understood. We took Stasia too. But that didn't slow her down. When she found out that Alex had gotten pregnant by some boy, she wanted to get pregnant too. That's when her dad grounded her and there were nasty words between the men."

"The night of the party I only remember bits and pieces. We got there safely, thanks to Stasi. Alex had already been doing whatever drug she did at the time, to get relaxed for the party."

"Did Stasia…..?"

"NO!! We never did that with her! Alex dabbled into too much stuff! She had a nickname for all of the ones she took, and Stasi saw how weird they would make her act. We were guilty of drinking and messing around, but not the pill popping."

"That's a relief! Did she die quick?"

"I don't know. I fell asleep in the backseat. I regret not insisting and calling a cab for us to get home safely. We didn't want to call our parents, because we were all reeking of alcohol. Stasi threw up a couple of times from being so full. We knew we messed up, and we took it upon ourselves to ride it out. A poor choice. Alex wanted me to drive, since I was the most 'sober drunk' out of all of us, but I couldn't walk a straight line, and my sense of direction was shot."

"Thank you for at least trying. That Alex was the devil! I remember hearing about the accident on the TV. It just didn't register that the car was Alex's. When Eric Dailey came to the door with the news I couldn't….."

"I understand. Stasia wouldn't want to see you like this. She visited me."

"Visited you?"

"She wanted me to let you know that she was sorry. Something about an event that happened before the party."

"She wasn't supposed to have went. She sneaked out of the house. Told us that she was going to empty the garbage and get ready for bed. When we went to her room to say good night she had already gone. Her father was livid! He was going to send her to his sister's house in another state. That's how much he hated her being around Alex. He wanted to get her away from 'the poison'."

"How is he taking it?"

"Hard. He goes to Alex's gravesite every day and pisses on it. One day her father caught him and they got to fighting right there at the cemetery. My husband was arrested, and didn't care. Her father put out a restraining order, so even though our children are both buried here he can only visit Stasia when he's not here which is what he should have been doing in the first place."

They sat there at her gravesite watching the leaves fall. Mrs. Webster pulled her close and hugged her. "Tell my baby that I love her with all my heart! And I think about her all day every day!"

"I will. Maybe her spirit can rest knowing that at least you're not angry with what she did. The men of these families and my mother are going to need a little more work."

"We were mean to your mother when we found out that you survived. The men were mean to her since the times of Fannie Gray. When I saw how mangled that car was and your arm dangling out in the picture I lost it. I never imagined how your mother felt. I'll admit that I wished that you died with them, but that wasn't the case. All while you were in a coma we did mean things to her. Made her hate us. We were all angry that you survived. Put a target on her like she was a criminal. She didn't deserve that from us, and we were such close friends before this. I would tease her about her keeping the church pews hot, she would say that she's keeping them warm for when we would come join her. Does she still go to church like that?"

"No. She's stopped going. She's so angry, defensive. When Mr. Peterson shot me I thought that she was going to blow the house up. It's too much, too heavy of a burden for one person to bear."

"True. It is. We're better than that, or at least we were supposed to be."

They got up and looked at Stasia's grave. Her mother left first towards her car. As she turned to leave a cold wind passed by her face causing Angelica to turn back around. There she saw Stasia standing by her grave. She looked at her, not saying a word. She saw Stasia smile and disappear. She turned around and headed toward the bus stop outside of the cemetery. She felt a little relieved, but she knew that she had a long way to go. She hoped and prayed while on the bus that her mother and Mrs. Webster would sit down and talk.

Mr. Peterson and Mr. Webster were both harder cases. Mr. Peterson was being held on attempted murder charges, and Mr. Webster just had become an angry man after his daughter died. As she got off of the bus she saw her again, the old woman standing on the other side of the street. She walked toward her; she knew that she had something to tell her. When she arrived at her destination the woman disappeared. She looked up to see that she was in front of her home. She noticed that the house looked different—bare. She went up to the door to see her mother packing things down.

She wanted to say something, but just kept silent. She knew why her mother was packing, she was tired. She turned around to go back down the walkway when she was stopped in her tracks. She turned around again and faced the house. She walked back inside the house and stopped in front of her mother. Her mother noticed her standing and looked up. The look on her face was that of distress. She looked at her, not saying a word. Her mother eased away from her. Angelica broke the silence. "Why are you moving?"

"We're moving and starting over somewhere else. Somewhere where there's kind people and Christians."

"There are kind people and Christians here. Where is your faith?"

"My faith is deep rooted. It hasn't went anywhere."

"It has. It's gone. That's why it's so easy for you to pack up and leave."

"How dare you tell me that my faith is gone! You never believed in God!"

"I believed, just didn't know how to apply it."

"So now since you've survived a car crash you know it all?!"

"No, I remember what you taught me. That's why I don't understand all this moving around. We moved when dad died, now you're on the move again because of how the people are treating me."

"I want peace!"

"Then ask for it, and receive it. Your heart is so hard, so full of negative things that you can't receive what is positive. And you think that by moving again that you'll find it."

"I will! We'll start anew, and you'll see."

"You'll start anew. I won't. I'm not running anymore. I'm going to face whatever it is that is coming at me."

"You'll move when I say you move!"

"Is it because of Fannie Gray's hold of this town that we're moving? Or is it really because of how the Peterson and Weber families have done?"

"You.....Fannie Gray? Who the hell told you about her? You don't need to know anything about her!"

Angelica had never heard her mother curse. She wished that she would tell her about this woman that her very name seemed to hit a nerve in her mother.

"No disrespect, but I can't. I have to finish here. You know that as well as I."

"We're moving and that's it!!" Her mother stormed off to another room. Angelica began to pray. Her mother came back to the room to see her on her knees praying. Anger swelled in her heart—*pray all you want to, I'm getting out of this town full of devils to a peaceful place! The evil here reminds me of the story of Lot.* Angelica got up and walked out of the door. Her mother called out to her, but her cries fell on deaf ears. She followed where the spirit led her. It was to the Weber house. Mrs. Weber hadn't made it home from her rounds, and Mr. Weber was sitting on the front porch.

He saw Angelica and began to shoo her away. She yelled out to him, "She wants you to not be angry at her foolishness!"

"Get away from my house before I do what old man Peterson couldn't do!!"

Angelica walked toward the porch, and Mr. Weber grabbed his pistol. "I told you that I'll kill you dead! She sat down and began singing. The song must had hit a nerve because Mr. Weber's hands began to shake. He looked at her trying to keep his hands steady for the shot. Then the tears came. He had the pistol at his side while he sobbed. "Please stop singing that song. It's too much to hear after everything that's happened."

Angelica couldn't help it, but sang even more. *It is well....in my soul....it is well, it is well....in my soul.* Mr. Weber sat down on his porch reduced to tears. Angelica walked up to him and dried his face on her shirt. "Don't cry Mr. Weber."

"You don't understand. They sang that song when my brother and his wife passed away in an accident off of a highway in Kentucky. The last thing that he said to me was how much he had turned his life around. He'd stopped partying and drinking, he stopped cheating on his wife. They had been through counseling and was renewing their vows. They joined church some months prior, and he would always sing pieces of that song. Said that he understood it."

"I see. The words are really deep. Guess it means something different to each person that hears it."

"What does it mean to you?"

"I was just delivering a message. Never knew all the words to the song. Guess it was meant for you. I spoke with your wife. I was visiting Stasia. I feel so alone and out of place here. She had a message for you and your wife. She's sorry for sneaking out and going to the party. She felt that if she'd obeyed you that she'd still be living."

"She would have, but hanging around with that strumpet Alex she was destined to stay in some type of trouble. I hated that girl, but she thought she was good as gold. Fool's gold."

"We just wanted to be popular. It sucks to be seen as all geeky and nerdy. When she paid us attention we sucked it up. We wanted to be popular like her. We wanted to be her."

"But why? The girl was a slut. She slept around to get things she wanted. Why would two smart girls like you and my Stasia want to dirty yourselves like that?"

"Boys. We wanted to have the cute ones on our arms. But we knew that they were looking for us to do the same things that Alex did. The farthest I went was kissing. My mother would kill me if she found out that I wasn't a virgin. But there was some guys that got real close."

"Was my Stasia….."

"No, she caved in. She cried about it for days afterward. I remember Alex telling her to suck it up, and that she just stepped into the big leagues."

If only they both knew that long before she went to the parties with Alex that Mr. Peterson had took her virginity a years earlier when she was 13.

"Bitch! Big leagues my ass!"

"She looked at me after Stasia lost her virginity, and doubled the efforts to have guys come at me. My mother shut that down quickly, telling them that if they tried that she would charge them with statutory rape. Almost shot me out for having a date for prom."

"Two points for your mother! She knew that the girl was a slut and protected you, protected you like I should have done for my Stasia. Now she's gone!"

"Have comfort in knowing that she never would want to see you cry because of her. She wished that she would have sided with me and taken the cab home, but we wanted to show all of you that we were responsible enough to get back home safely. I should have never went at all."

Mrs. Weber came up the walkway to see Angelica talking with her husband. She slowed here pace toward him, not knowing what his state of mind was. He signaled to her, and she walked towards him leery of what to expect. Once by her husband, he pulled her down and hugged her, crying. Angelica moved out of the way for they could sit side by side. "It's time for you two to heal. Stasia's gone, but she wouldn't want to see you two at each other's throats. It disturbs her. She wants you to remember her the way she was before the accident....before Alex. I'm thinking about doing something special in her memory, but I don't know what."

"She liked flowers," Mrs. Weber said, "We would do the front and back of the house every year. She loved yellow blooms."

"Then maybe we can plant some yellow flowers at her favorite spot in town."

"That would be nice, "her father joined in. "And we'll have all yellow blooms in the garden this year. In remembrance."

She took her leave humming as she left. They both looked at her and smiled. Angelica was humming The Yellow Rose of Texas, a song that they danced to when they were dating. She walked on to the bus stop where she was met by a classmate of hers. She greeted him, but received less than a nice reply. "You were never in that car, you bailed out before they crashed. That's how you survived it all. You never liked Alex, and she knew it!"

"I was in the back seat sleep. Pictures don't lie."

"You are a murderer! You set them up to die! You were mad that I wouldn't give you the time of day and let them die!"

"I don't know who you are, and I wasn't about dating any guys anyway. I was looking forward to leaving here and going to college. You were Alex's boyfriend, but that didn't stop you from trying to hit on Stasia. You wanted her more than you did Alex."

"Liar! I loved Alex!"

"And Trisha, and Carmen, and Julie, and Carol....you loved everybody!"

He scooped Angelica up by her neck, "Listen bitch, you're not liked around here. You or your witch of a mammy. The best thing that you can do is to get your ass out of this town!"

"I'm not moving. Got work to do."

"You'll move, or be without a house!" he threw her down on the sidewalk and walked off. She dusted herself off. Had her mother had similar threats? She headed toward home. This madness had to come to an end. She entered her mother's house to see her on the ground beat up and bleeding.

"Mama!! Are you alright?"

"They.....they.....run...RUN!!!" Then the lights went out. She awoke to the rain hitting her face. Where was her mother? Where was she? She shook her head trying to focus to see if where she was familiar. The place was dark, and she was tied to a pole. Was it nighttime? Was she outside somewhere? She heard crackling. Was someone near a fire somewhere? She tuned her ear to see if she could hear anything to identify where she had been taken. She just hoped and prayed that her captors had left her mother alone. They wanted her—they all wanted her. All she could do was pray; she was fearful for her mother's life. After all she was packing to leave town, why the attack? Who was really behind all of this hatred?

The lights blinded her. She smelled the gasoline. Cars? Trucks? She was indeed outside, and whoever had brought her here wasn't planning on her leaving here alive. Then she heard him....it couldn't be.....Eric? What was he doing here? Was he here to save her? What was going on? Her heart raced, as she didn't know the answers to her questions. She pleaded in her mind and heart with God. *Please Father, make a way!! This is not your way or your doing!! Please help us!!*

She could hear Eric fussing at someone in the distance. Whoever he or she was Eric wasn't pleased at the results that he had been given. A radio was set in the place where Angelica was, tuned to the local station. *In local news the fire department is rushing to contain a fire at 644 Maplewood Street. The fire department is trying their best to see if there was anyone inside of the house, but at this time they cannot say whether or not the inhabitants a Ms. Angelica Carroll or her mother were inside. More details as we receive updates....in other news.....*

Angelica's heart sank. She knew. They torched the house and left her mother inside. She cried silently, praying that her mother's soul would find peace. It didn't matter what these people would do to her now. They all reminded her of Sodom and Gomorrah. Sinful people that didn't care about it at all. How was she to save a town or do whatever she was meant to do under such hard circumstances? What was she to do now? The truth would be spun around and she would be the villain again. She knew it. How would she prove her innocence this time? Or was it her time?

She calmed her mind and braced herself for whatever her captors had in mind for her. They had done the worst, they had killed her mother in pure hatred. Why didn't they just kill her like they wanted to instead? She heard footsteps outside of the lights. Then a voice. It wasn't Eric's or Alex's boyfriend, it was someone unfamiliar. Just as fast as the lights were on they were off again, but the voice was still there. "So you are the one who cheated death?" She remained silent. "You're the one who cannot be killed by bullets at close range. You're the one who everyone in this town either is afraid of or hates. But I'll soon fix that, just like I fixed your mother! No words?"

Angelica sensed something purely evil. The voice was purely evil.

She remained silent, and honed in her inner voice to block out the words that were being said. The voice sensed that he wasn't getting through and yelled at her, "Pray all you want, you won't leave here alive!! And in death you'll join me, like your friends in that car are!! His laugh made the hair on the back of her neck stand up. "I'll have such fun torturing you before you die!! And these townsfolk all will help me do it, like they did your mother. She never knew what hit her!! Blow after blow! They howled at her crawling across the floor trying to get away! Wonder if she cried out to God to save her? Isn't that what you're doing right now? Won't help. Didn't help her."

She remained quiet still, listening now, gathering information on who this person was. He was a pure evil person, almost demonic. He was gone out of the space they shared, and she was left alone. She fell asleep, not knowing where she was, but also not fearing the future. If this person had this much power to sway the minds of a town then God would truly have to come into this town to fight. Hours later she was woke up to the sunlight in her face and her at another location. Had she been moved during the night? It didn't matter. She knew where she was at. She was on the edge of town at the old abandoned Gray's place. They had died off decades ago under 'strange' circumstances. Rumor was that the wife practiced in black magic, and when her husband found out he left her. She never cried a tear, but a year later he came back to her. Months after that he died, and she never changed expression. There was never any funeral for her husband, no body of her husband ever found, and no burial plot. It was as if he vanished off the earth. It wasn't until her death two decades later that the town got the answers they feared. Her husband's few remaining bones were found in the pig sty. And she was revealed as a heavy student of the black arts. They said that a lot of books were found at the house. But where were those books now? Who had them? Could the man behind the voice have them?

She was stood up in the yard of the house. Her captors were clothed in black and red, faces covered, but it was a given that they were local townsfolk. Who else would do it? She looked up and around, unfazed at it all. How could her mother not know about the demonic influence of this town? Or did she know and fought against it? She couldn't ask her now about it, she had to face this evil by herself. The crowd gathered around, taking seats anywhere they could on the property. The voice stood several feet in front of her, and looked at her in disgust. He stayed covered from head to toe, unlike the others who just wore masks to distort their faces.

"Still silent? Still praying? Won't help you here." Angelica looked at the voice and smiled.

"Ah, a smile. Or should I say a smirk!" She smiled even bigger. That seemed to enrage the demon under the costume. "I have to hand it to you, you're nothing like your mother! I beat her with my bare hands!! Told her to call out to her God to save her! In the end she became boring, and he never came. Maybe he'll come for you."

She looked at him. And all of a sudden the words came. "Demon, why don't you show yourself!! Show these lost souls of yours how you really look!"

Enraged at what was said he signaled for the two men to let her go. "I can kill you here and now!"

"The body is nothing but a shell. You cannot kill my spirit!! But yours is doomed for eternity!! And so are theirs!!"

There was a low mumble from the crowd. She smiled even brighter. You came here through Mrs. Gray. My mother knew about her evil, and how various townsfolk would come through here for potions for all kinds of things. She knew all about her."

More mumbles. The voice hissed. "Now it's your time to meet your maker!" He came at her with such force that the men that were standing besides her were on the ground several feet away. However, Angelica hadn't budged an inch. She looked at him unaverred. The voice was enraged. She was stronger than her mother. It would take more. He looked around to see the townspeople slowly disappearing. They had become afraid. They scattered out from the house to their cars, leaving the voice to whatever he was going to do with Angelica. Those that remained were there just to see the outcome, or were too scared to move. Some of them revived by the power of the voice took off their masks to reveal who they were and urged him on. None of that mattered to Angelica, this evil had to be killed before it took all the souls of this town that didn't know what was going on.

The voice looked at her and laughed. "So you think you're tough? Think that you can take me down? You don't know who you're dealing with!!"

"The spawn of Satan? A demon of some level or another? Someone that's been in black magic and the arts so long that their soul is black?"

The voice looked at her in pure hatred and whipped off his hood to show his face. There stood Marlon Peterson. The remaining townsfolk that were there cheered him on as if he was the starting quarterback of their favorite team. She stood there unfazed. Marlon Peterson. What ties did he have to this old house? To the Grays? He looked at her almost hissing as he spoke to her. "I knew when you survived that accident what you were. I'm not a demon, YOU ARE!! Just like your mother was! Old Mrs. Gray knew it too! How else could you explain all the things that your mother did over the years?"

He looked at her. She didn't know. He laughed at her loss of words. "You didn't know!!" He laughed even harder. "That will be what I'll have them put on your grave, if they leave enough of you to bury!!"

"I knew. I knew about Mrs. Gray. I knew what she was doing in this house. How she killed her husband for trying to get away from her and her evil magic. How she would hold meetings here for her followers. I knew."

"She did all of the rituals to get rid of your mother and her black magic!"

"Lies of the devil!!" She felt her face heat up. She was tired of all the talk, and she wanted him to take his best shot.

"Your God won't stop me from killing you, just like he's never stopped me from killing all of those that were against Mrs. Gray! She saved my life and my family's life many times!"

"In exchange for your soul. Pathetic. Hope it was worth it."

"She was an angel! She fought against people like you who come here deceiving the world!!" He began to speak an incantation. Then the weather changed. Angelica never looked up, just looked at him. It made sense. He had the books from Mrs. Gray. He had been practicing here all this time. She stood her ground amid the weather changes and looked him square in the eye. Then she noticed the lights and corrected her stance. They were getting brighter as they neared her. Puzzled to why Angelica was staring off and his remaining followers standing with fear on their faces, he turned around as the light neared him. He covered his face and the other followers made a hasty retreat, or tried. The light covered the area, over her, and kept on past her. As it passed over her it was warm like the sun.

As she looked in front of her she saw Marlon Peterson. Was he still alive? She could hear the faint screams and squeals of cars speeding off in the distance. She walked slowly towards Marlon, not knowing what to expect when she was stopped in her tracks by the old woman. "No need to tend to him. Go back to the town."

"But...."

"All your questions are soon to be answered. Go there."

How was she to get there? She had been brought out here by Marlon's henchmen. As she walked away toward the glades she saw the car that one of the followers left behind with the keys in the ignition. She started the car and headed toward town, not really knowing whether she was heading into a lynch mob or everybody shunning her like they did her mother. As she drove off the old woman looked at Marlon Peterson. "For so long you were indeed given chances to change. Instead you took up the cause of this witch and lost your soul. You never told your wife of what really happened to your sons or your daughter. You lived lies trying to harness the power of evil to no avail. Now you must pay!!"

"No!! I didn't know she was....." All Angelica saw from the forest area was a flash. All she could think was all this time he practiced that evil for power. Did his wife know? She couldn't have. Did she see something that scared her into keeping her distance from him? She drove into town to see the remains of her house. She went up to the house. Mrs. Peterson came behind her. "Thank God you're ok!! Where is your mother?"

"She may be in there. I don't know. I know that some townsfolk had beat her up real bad, and when I went to help her I ended up by the Gray house outside town."

"I thought that they burned that place down. They should have! That woman was evil!"

Angelica had to know if her mother was in the house when they torched it. She went through rubble, careful not to step on glass or anything. Mrs. Peterson soon came behind her to try and help. The police chief soon came up and yelled to them. Angelica sensed that she was close to something when he started yelling for them to come out of the house. Mrs. Peterson came out, but Angelica drawn to go on went in further. The police chief threatened to come in and arrest her if she didn't come out. She kept on until she stopped short of the kitchen. There she found her, crawling for the back door. She held her head down and said a prayer for her. They didn't even bother to take her body out of the house. The police chief came in and stopped in his tracks. He backed up and became quiet as she walked out with her mother's charred body. Mrs. Peterson cried out loud at the sight. She laid her mother in the cool grass and covered her over.

She looked up at the police chief, "Happy at your work? This was done by your hand!! You followed Mr. Peterson, in fact you let him out of jail! You are a murderer!!"

"I did nothing of the sort! I was in the office all day!"

"And you let my mother die in a house that she couldn't get out of. Even if she had reached the back door you all jammed it where she couldn't get out." A crowd had gathered and began to whisper. "You murdered my mother because she was against your town witch!!" The murmurs became louder as the crowd grew bigger. Those that had seen the lightshow earlier were not there in the crowd, but these were people that stayed in the town to themselves.

"I didn't do this, you did!"

"You also had a hand from preventing me to go and get help. The person who snatched me from behind I managed to scratch his arms up with my nails. I see the scratches Chief." He pulled his gun out and pointed it towards her. "You're the witch, just like your mother was. This town was peaceful before you two came here!"

"This town was evil led by a witch living on your outskirts of town. She did all kinds of things to the people of this town by request. Everyone here has lost something or someone because of her. Pets, cars, jobs, houses, lovers, children. She worked her magic to the request of you mean, jealous hearted people of this town!"

Mrs. Weber looked to the Chief. "Is this true? Did you do this to her mother? Did you?!" One of the football players knocked the gun out of his hand and ripped the sleeve of his shirt. "Look there are the scratches! She didn't lie! You killed her mother!!"

The chief backed up and started to run. He didn't get far before he was tackled in the street. None of that would bring her mother back. She sat by her mother's body. She didn't deserve to die the way she did. It should have been her. She hoped that her work was done. She laid by her mother's body wishing to be held once more and cried. The townspeople were now a mob of good versus evil with ropes and guns. She looked up to see all the discord. How was she going to stop this mess? She stood up and felt weak. She sat back down hoping to regain some strength.

She noticed a glimmer. She followed it to two safe boxes. They had cooled enough for her to take them out of the house. The Webers provided her with shelter until she got in touch with her relatives. She opened the first locked box to see nothing but letters about various townspeople and the favors that they had asked for. Some asked for positions of power which the payment was various sums of money. Some of the names shocked her. Eric? He asked the witch for something? She read the letter about him. Favors for wealth, position. She thought that he was smarter than that. She looked through all the names. She saw Mrs. Weber's name and what she asked for. Her heart sank. She took the note and closed the box. Once alone, she gave the note to her. She held her head down. The second box contained the books the shaman gave her mother years ago.

"I wanted answers to why my husband didn't want me. I asked her to do potions to make him love me again. It didn't work."

"Here's why." Angelica gave the letter to his widow. She read it and cried.

"How did you find this out?"

"My mother did."

"Wait this isn't addressed to my husband. It's......its...... Marlon......oh my God!! What did he do to my daughter?"

She left the note with her to read. She knew the note would provide no solace, but the truth was finally beginning to come out about the people of the town and how wicked they were. She went back and read a few more letters that her mother wrote about the townspeople. The chief was the next letter she read. His favors were that of power and control. He wanted control over his officers, and for the town to not have hardened criminals like the towns around them. He saw the drugs coming in, and got his hands dirty almost getting caught. That was where Fannie came in. She gave him protection.

Then she read Eric's. How he loved Alex and she constantly blew him off. He didn't want to be seen as 'her big brother' he wanted to be her man—her only man. When she began to develop and take an interest in boys he became more protective of her than her dad did, and with good reason—he wanted her for himself. He went to Fannie for something to sway her to him, and Fannie laughed at him. Her thoughts were interrupted by a knock on the Weber's door. It was Eric. He was looking for her. Before Mrs. Weber could open the door to the room Angelica was there.

"You want me. You want to kill me."

"I just want to talk to you."

"No, you don't. I have this letter about you. About your lust for Alex Peterson. I guess you're pissed at me because of what you think my mother did years ago!"

"Your mother killed an upstanding woman!"

"Fannie Gray was evil, and did evil things to this town and everyone in it. You haven't figured it out yet?"

Eric pulled his gun and motioned for her to come towards him. Mr. and Mrs. Weber backed away. "You'll take me to Marlon Peterson, he'll know what to do with you!!"

"He's dead. I can take you to his remains. He's not too far from where his sister died. She really did a number on this town!"

"Marlon's sister stays in another state!"

"He had two sisters. They both stayed out of state, but one he was close to the other one he wasn't. Guess which one came to visit."

Eric grabbed her and walked her out to the car. Angelica didn't resist him and sat in the car. Eric was red faced with anger. "Things were fine until you and your mother came here! Your mother constantly fought with Mrs. Fannie!"

"My mother did no such thing. For all the evil Fannie did for the townspeople my mother did the opposite. She dealt with healing people from colds and diseases. Sure she knew all about Fannie, she came to my mother and told her to stop doing good or move out of town. That the town was her territory to possess not hers. My mother didn't come to this town to claim territory or possess anything or anyone just to live and get out lives back to normal after the loss of my dad. It was Fannie who declared war on my mother and used all of you to do it, even after her death."

"Lies!!"

"Did her potion work for you? Did Alex fall madly in love with you like you wanted?"

Eric slapped Angelica across the face. "I don't like your smart mouth!"

"I take that to mean no. Shame. Seems like everyone else got a turn on that one!"

"Shut up bitch! Just get ready to get the punishment that demons get! Marlon will kill you and rid the town of you!!"

Angelica looked out of the window for the rest of the ride. Fannie had made sure to brainwash many of the people here in the town.

Olive Weber showed the note to her husband. He read it, and looked at her. "Who gave this to you? Did you read what that sick fucker did to our daughter? He even impregnated her! I'll kill him!!"

Mr. Weber went to the Peterson household gun in hand. Mrs. Weber went in behind him, hoping to calm him down and talk him out of it. She didn't want any more bloodshed. Mr. Weber drove up to the Petersons house and got out of the car. He didn't bother to turn it off he was so determined to get out and het hold to Marlon. He went up to the door bamming on it until Mrs. Peterson came down. She opened the door and looked at her. "Where is that rapist of a husband of yours? Got some words for him."

"I haven't seen him in three days. Put out a police report. Not like him. Last I knew he was going out to his sister's place to get it ready to sell."

"Liar! Where is that rapist of a husband of yours? No need to hide him from me! I'll tear your house to pieces to find him!"

"He's not here! What are you talking about rape? Who did my husband…..?"

Mr. Weber pushed Mrs. Peterson aside. Mrs. Weber showed Mrs. Peterson the note. It all made sense. She held her head down in shame. He impregnated Anastasia? She was younger than their daughter. Was that what he had Fannie do for him? It would explain the times when she would turn over in the bed at night what he was doing.

Eric escorted Angelica down the stairs of the house and to his car. In the rush to get her to his car Angelica dropped Eric's envelope along with a duplicate of Marlon's on the doorstep. Eric looked at Angelica once they drove off towards Fannie Gray's house. "He's there becoming more powerful for he can become mayor of the town. We're done with how this one we have is running things!"

Angelica stayed silent. She knew that Marlon was gone. Destroyed by the bright light that caused the ground to shake. She hoped that the books were destroyed with him. Too much evil in them. They pulled up to Fannie's house. Eric yanked Angelica out of the car and chained her to the post they originally had for her to be burned at. He looked around, calling out to Marlon. Then the smell hit him. Burnt flesh smell. He followed the smell to the spot where he saw what was left of Marlon—his badly burned shoes and the pendant that he wore melted on his skeleton.

Eric looked around to see where the book was he was holding. If he could find it he could be the most powerful man in town like

Marlon had become. He could have any woman he wanted, riches, even kill off those that opposed him. He went back to the place where he had Angelica chained to see that she had escaped. Did she know where the books were? Did she have the books? He searched the house to see if she was in there. "Angelica! I know you're in here! Come out! I know that you have the books! Give them to me! I've earned them! This cursed town owes me, and everyone in it!"

Angelica was nowhere near the house, and didn't have the books. She was freed by the old woman that she had seen in town. "Go away from here! This place will be destroyed. Go away!"

"What about the books he's talking about? Don't they need to be destroyed? Where are they?"

"They have been destroyed. The last one burned with the man over there. Your mother destroyed the rest."

"What about the other evil men and women of this town?"

"They will all die off. Leave now!"

Angelica ran toward Eric's car to see that he took his keys with him. She continued on out of the woods to the highway. Fannie's house was so far out she would be walking for quite some time to get back to town. She felt the earth shaking again. She felt the hairs on the back of her neck stand up. She wasn't far away enough!! She ran as fast as she could down the back road to get away. She saw the light in the corner of her eye, but she kept running ahead. From the glimpse she got of it was brighter than the one before that enveloped her and Marlon, killing him and sparing her.

Eric turned books over and tables. "They have to be here! Where did he hide those books?"

"What you seek has been destroyed." The old woman replied.

Eric looked up to her. "They have not! He hid them to keep the power all to himself! Selfish bastard! I won't stop until I find them!"

"You will stop."

"I will not! Move out of my way old woman!" Eric pushed the woman out of the way.

"This house will be destroyed with everything in it. Such evil cannot be allowed to exist."

Eric annoyed at the woman's remark turned to take a hit at her to find her gone. *That was her best bet. Would have given her one right between her eyes.* He noticed that the sun was shining…..no it couldn't be this bright. It was 4 in the afternoon…..the light was getting brighter. He felt hot in his uniform as if the temperature outside was 110 degrees. He wiped the sweat from his brow and went tried to go toward the desk. His shoes were sticking to the floor. The light seemed to surround the house. Items on the wall were catching fire or melting. He couldn't get out. He tried to sum up a way to make a dash for a door or window, but was overcome by flames.

Angelica fell some miles up from exhaustion. While not in the immediate radius of the house she could still feel the intense heat from the flames. She laid on the roadway and closed her eyes. It was coming…she was finally going to be at rest.

"Harry what do they want us to do with that type of fire? I can feel the heat from here!"

"Whoa!"

"Whoa what?"

"Stop the truck. There's something in the road."

Lewis and Harry stopped the truck. Lewis turned Angelica over. "She's still alive! Call for a medic to come get her!"

Harry radioed in for the paramedics, but wondered what she was doing out here. This girl seemed to be at the wrong places at the wrong time. Lewis called for more fire trucks, but the ones from other towns had seen the fire and were caught at a dead end from the intense heat. He reported back to Harry. "This must be one hell of a fire! Some of the other engines tried to get to it and they're blocked too from the heat from it. No way in hell anything survived that!"

Harry wasn't concerned about the fire. He held Angelica in his arms. She looked up at him. He looked down at her. "The medics are comin' for you sweetheart. Everything's going to be alright."

She smiled. She remembered his voice from the accident. She was safe. When the paramedics arrived they tried to put her on the stretcher, but she wouldn't let go of Harry. Lewis came to see what the fuss was all about. "She won't let go of me."

"Then go with her! It's nothing we can do here until this fire dies down. It's not spreading anywhere, just super-hot like a volcano. May just go back to the station on this one."

Harry nodded and boarded the ambulance with Angelica. As they rode toward the town he noticed her looking at him. He smiled back at her. "We meet again."

All she could do was smile. She felt her strength leaving her body. She held his hand. He looked at her again. "Hey you guys you need to stop the bleeding!!"

The medic in the back looked in shock. "She wasn't bleeding when we picked her up!" The medic got right to work trying to stop the bleeding. As they got into the hospital doors more bruises appeared on Angelica's body. Harry followed her inside until he wasn't allowed to go any further. He felt something wasn't quite right. It was her. Lewis radioed to Harry that they were able to get to the house and put the fire out. The old Gray place was leveled to the ground. He also said that there were several bodies exposed around and under the house. Harry looked for answers. What did this girl really know? Where did all her wounds come from?

As she laid there on the table the doctor's voices sounded muffled. Was her mission finished? She felt the strength leaving her body. The room fell silent. She opened her eyes to darkness. Where was she? What was she lying on? Then she heard voices. "That girl has more lives than a cat!" one voice said.

"Well, I wouldn't want to be in her shoes. So much loss. Does she have any relatives? I haven't heard about anyone coming from her family to take her."

"I don't think she has anyone. That's the reason that the Webers' took her in. And now her for her to take her dead mother out of a burnt house..."

Harry waited to hear some kind of news about Angelica. When the doctor came out he stood up. "She's going to pull through. What happened to her? Who shot and beat her?"

"We just found her in the road outside the old Gray house."

"That woman and her kin was bad news."

"Yeah, she was. Can I see her?"

"She's sleeping, but when she awakes she'll probably be glad to see you."

Harry went on home, glad that Angelica was alright, but with more questions than answers. As he drove to his house he noticed the small things that had changed in the town. Gone was the older stores replaced with more modern superstores. There were no kids playing out anymore—they were all adults now and had moved away. The town had become old. The deaths of Alexandra and Anastasia uncovered more than it cured. Their deaths were the only easy thing about the town. Who knew that Fannie Gray was Marlon's sister, and that she did so many heinous things to and for people?

And to think that after her death instead of letting the town and its people heal, that he took it upon himself to try to be as powerful as she was. Now where the house stood was leveled to the ground as if lava had covered everything over. And the bodies!! Lewis had told him that once they were able to put the fire out, they found remains of over 30 people around the house. Had she been killing people all these years? How much of the rumors were true? He pulled into the driveway of his home. His wife peeked out of the door to see if it was him. She looked at his worn-down face. She was just glad to see him.

He came in and his wife asked him about coffee. "No thank you."

"Is the young girl ok?"

"Yeah, I don't think she has any family left though. No one's come to even check on her. A young girl all alone in the world."

"So what are they going to do with her? Where will she go? Is she old enough to take care of herself?"

"Honey, I don't know. All I know is that all these years how could a whole town be so blind and corrupt? Who knew that Fannie Gray was Marlon's sister?"

"I did."

"Huh? You did?"

"Yeah. There were four of them in the beginning. Two boys, Marlon and Burt, and two girls Fannie and Penny. The family had always been strange from the beginning."

"Strange how?"

"Well, it all started with Burt. He was born disabled, and their father blamed it on their mother. Would beat her something terrible. She never came out. After a while neither did Burt."

"What do you mean? The kids did go to school didn't they?"

"Everyone but Burt. You know the disability thing. Peterson was embarrassed by him. I remember one time when we were at church and the poor boy had a seizure, he said it was from the devil. Told the preacher to remove the demon. He dragged the boy clear up to the altar in full seizure and dropped him there. The crowd was in full shock."

"I bet. So seems like Burt was an epileptic. Why didn't the preacher call the ambulance? Get some help for the boy?"

"It was a mess. Imagine seeing all the ruckus as a child."

"So what happened?"

"His father was so insistent on the preacher getting rid of the 'demon' that he dared anyone to move. The boy died right there."

"Oh my God! No one tried to help the boy?"

"Old man Peterson was a man that was feared. After Burt died there in the church he wasn't seen again."

"But what of his wife and kids?"

"They were only allowed to go to school for a few more years after that. Only rumors of what was happening in that house after that. Penny was the only one that broke away from them, and by what I heard she had to smuggle herself out of that house with the trash."

"What? What do you mean smuggle? They were going to school…..I don't understand."

"After Burt's death, Peterson started worshipping the devil. Didn't hide the fact much either. But not everyone was trying to see what he was doing in that house. Rumor has it that he killed the wife off and was sleeping with the daughters."

"So the wife died?"

"I think so. Never heard from her after they made him bury Burt."

"Made him?"

"Yep. He wanted no parts of him when the preacher couldn't get rid of his 'demon'. He told the police that they could do whatever they wanted to 'it', that his son was dead way before that happened."

Harry saw how choked up his wife was getting telling the story. He held her close. "I don't want to hear anymore. God, I don't."

His wife cried in his arms. He could only imagine seeing all this as a child, in a church at that. He also understood why his wife stopped going. Seeing a memory like that he probably would have stopped going too. He remembered that they didn't get married in the church. They had the mayor marry them in city hall. Explained quite a bit as to why over the years that the church was barely open. He left his wife to her chores. Old man Peterson a devil worshipper? Penny having to smuggle herself out of town? He wanted to get to the bottom of what happened to the town—it was almost a compulsion.

The Webers hoped for good news for Angelica. They had found that she had family from her mother's side, and were awaiting to hear from them. Perhaps they would let her stay with them until she was healed up to make it on her own. The girl had been through so much that it was time for her family to step up. They were going through their own problems and didn't want the burden of housing her for the long term.

Angelica woke up sore and looking around. She was in the hospital. *Well, I guess I don't get to die today…*she thought to herself. She found herself more tired mentally than physically. Just over the course of a year she had lost two close friends, cheated death, and lost her mother in a town that was so evil that everywhere she turned she saw it. She sat up on the side of the bed. What was she going to do now? She had no place to go, no job, and no family. She sat on the side of her bed and cried. What was her mission now? Marlon Peterson was dead along with several of his followers in a 'fire' that still had people from surrounding towns talking. She could hear bits and pieces of conversations—"the fire was so hot that it took the firemen 8 hours before they could get near the flames" "they found over fifty bodies buried" "only charred remains of thirty" "ground so hot that the firemen's shoes were sticking to the ground". As she sat on the side of the bed she thought to herself, *if only they really knew what happened there. It sure wasn't any fire, that's for sure. It was God's wrath.*

The nurse and doctor came into see Angelica. The doctor spoke first. "How are you feeling?"

"Sore. How long have I been here?"

"Four days. Almost lost you. You lost a lot of blood. There were some police officers wanting to question you."

She was surprised that there were any left. Most of the policemen were caught in the first blast. She was surprised that the heat they talked about didn't harm the town. The nurse checked her vitals. She looked at her like she was some type of weird specimen. "Why are you looking at me like that?"

The nurse stepped back. "Looking at you like what?"

"Like something's odd or wrong."

The doctor stepped in to the nurse's defense. "What do you remember?"

She sat up. She had been here with these questions before. She looked out of the window. "Nothing."

She remembered it all. How Eric wanted her to give her Fannie Gray's books and drug her to the old Gray house—or what was left of it—for her to give up the books. The books had been destroyed—the last one in Marlon Peterson's hands when the first wave came through, the others when Fannie and her mother fought. She didn't trust any of them anymore. The doctor walked out to continue his rounds. The nurse stood there looking at her.

"What is it? You want to ask me something."

"How do you do it?"

"Do what?"

"Hide your wings. How do you hide them for other people can't see them?"

"I don't have wings."

"Yes you do. I can see them. Some people say that I have them. Can you see mine?"

Angelica was irritated. Wings. Halos. Some people were just nuts.

She looked at the nurse in anger, but she saw something. Something glowing behind the nurse's back. What was going on?

"You can see mine!" She went up and hugged her so tight that she thought she was going to squeeze the air out of her. "Will come see you after my shift!"

She wondered what just happened. She walked over to the window and looked out. What was going on? She saw something. And her grandmother coming to her? With the fires that had hit the town she wondered how there were any businesses let alone people left. She wanted to get out of the hospital and see what all was left. She went into the bathroom to see her wounds. Bandaged stomach area from the gunshot that came back weeks after it happened. Redness from burns on her knees, arms, and face. She rinsed her face off and removed the IV. She had to get out. This town and the remaining people here was driving her nuts. But where would she go? She got on her clothes and left the hospital. She had no idea of where she was going, but she wasn't going to submit to anymore questions. That time was over. They all knew what was going on, how they let evil in their town and closed their eyes to it. She wasn't strong enough to fight this battle. Once free, she ran as fast as her feet could carry her.

Running in the direction of where she used to stay she knew from there how to get out of the town. Once there at the remains she stopped and looked up to the sky. *Mama, I miss you so. I should have listened and left when you said that it was time to leave! But I had to be hard-headed! And it cost you your life! Mama, I'm so sorry!! Please forgive me!* After crying and letting it all out she went on about her way. She made up in her mind that she would put this evil town behind her once and for all. As she was running, wind in her hair, she was almost ran over by Harry in his car.

"Hey! I almost hit you!"

She corrected herself before taking off again. She hadn't heard a word he said, and kept running. Harry took off in pursuit of her, wondering where she was running off to. What had gotten into her to be running out of the town so fast? He had to push the car to its limits. How could she be running so fast? He was able to cut her off and stop her running. "Hey! Stop! I need to talk to you!"

Frantic, she had to get around this car and get away. Harry grabbed her by her shoulders and put her in a bear hug. "Stop! You're safe. You've ran out of town. Where are you going?"

She stopped and looked at him. It was the paramedic that had saved her in the beginning. She looked at him and cried as she returned the hug. He held her tight, knowing in part what all she had went through and defied the odds. She had no one but herself. The police in part killed her mother and then burned the house, other people were scared of her because of how she managed to survive bullets, and fires so hot that firemen couldn't put them out. As he held her she began to cry. He cried with her, for all her loss and for how a town destroyed her life.

As he walked her over to his car he looked at her eyes. She looked well rested, but still worried. He hoped that she wouldn't take off running again. Instead she held on to him tight.

"Get in. I'll take you home with me. You'll be alright there."

"Let me go. No one in that town wants me around. Most everybody left is scared of me, and I haven't done anything to anyone!"

"People are always scared of things they don't understand."

"And it's the nature of people to kill what they can't control."

"True. My wife told me about this town. This town was evil before you and your mother got here. I have some places my wife told me about that may make what you're going through make some type of sense."

"I just want to get out of this town!"

"And whatever you're being kept alive for to do won't let you leave! Have you noticed every time you try to leave things happen? No time in my life have I fought a fire so damn hot it took almost two days for any fire department to go into. And when we went there the bodies! Some burned to cinders others melted into the metal plates that were in the ground out there. We found the skeletons of over 30 people besides that! And only you survived! Yes! People will be scared of you!

And they're more scared because you've survived things that should have killed you. That's why they are scared of you!"

"I never asked for any of this! I know I should have died in the car accident!" she started crying again. "So much loss! Everyone's gone and I'm still here! My mom, my friends!"

"I know. But there's something special about you Angelica. Your mother saw it when you survived that accident. Just rest for tonight. Please. Tomorrow if you still want to leave I'll take you to the edge of town."

Angelica went home with Harry. Once there his wife was in the kitchen. She came out of the kitchen with her apron on. Angelica immediately recognized her. It was the lady that spoke to her on the bus stop. Henry's wife stood there hoping that Angelica wouldn't reveal to him that they had talked before. In her mind it was telling her to run, but her feet felt like cement and she couldn't move. She offered for her to sit down since it was close to time for dinner. She did, somewhat comfortable. Harry took off his coat and went to wash his hands. "Caught her walking from her old house."

"Why you're not in the hospital with those wounds? After you eat I'll clean those up for you. The bandages look like they need changing."

Angelica looked at Harry's wife. What a twist of fate. Maybe she could give her some direction and answer her questions as she had done before. As she looked at her she saw her wings, beautiful and white. She looked at Harry, he didn't have any, but had an aura around him. Were they dead and just here to guide her to what she needed to do? She wanted to say something, but the words escaped her. She sat down in their living room, and before she knew it fell asleep.

"Poor thing, she's tired. Fell asleep on the couch." Harry said.

"Let her be, she needs the rest." Said Maria, Harry's wife. "That girl is an angel just trying to get her wings."

"Aren't we all?"

Maria smiled, knowing deep inside that she had hers already. She was just waiting for her time to go. As she finished dinner her mind went back to when she was a young girl. She didn't disclose to her husband that she was captured by old man Peterson's followers. The very thought of all the girls they captured that summer—the ones that their parents didn't give outright to the cult—was shocking. She remembered the pleas of the girls begging for the men not to take their virginity. The screams of the girls being sodomized almost drove her crazy. She remembered two of the girls that was in the room with her. They looked at her in disgust.

"Why haven't they touched you? Why haven't they raped you?" one girl asked.

"I don't know!"

"Her folks must got money or something. I can't believe that my father gave me away to them! Ten men did whatever they wanted to me! Ten! And there you sit—untouched!" the other girl hissed.

They had a right to be angry. It was all beyond any of their control. If she could she would rescue all of the girls and tell them to run as fast as they could out of this town. One morning she overheard some of the men talking.

"This one killed herself. Bled out. Used the screws from the bed to dig into her wrists."

"Peterson will be pissed about that. Let's go tell him to see what he wants us to do with the body. Shame, she was a good lay. She had been well broken in. Could have been used."

The men walked off down the hallway out of earshot. The two girls that were in the room with her were also gone. Were the men using them again? This time it was quiet—the kind that made her uneasy. What was going on? She would soon find out. As the day wore on the room door opened. Standing in the doorway was a man in all red. She remembered the vibe she got from him. She scurried back into the corner, scared for her life. His dark eyes looked at her as he said "Come here."

Maria was scared stiff and couldn't move. The man in red said again, "Come here." She still cowered in the corner. The man again said, "COME HERE!!!" and it seemed like her body was lifted and thrown into his grasp. She didn't look him in the eyes in fear, but that didn't matter to him. He took her to a dressing room. There she saw some other girls she went to school with. They all hugged after the doors were closed. They exchanged information on how they got there. Apparently she wasn't the only one that was taken from their parents. Old man Peterson was busy. One girl said that it was almost as if he had the women of the town hypnotized. She saw a lot of her friends' mother's in the cult serving Peterson like he was their husband.

She knew that her mother wasn't going for anything like that. They were God-fearing bible thumpers. She asked if they had been raped by any of the men, and they said no. It was only six of them, six out of dozens of girls that didn't make the cut. Maria was snapped out of her thought by Harry asking her if she was cold.

"No dear, I'm not. Why you ask?"

"You have chill bumps on your arms."

She smiled, rubbed her arms and went back to the task she was doing. She dismissed the thought from her mind and finished dinner. Angelica felt a peace being here—as if she was safe here. Harry came back in to tell her that dinner would be ready and to wash her hands. Ironic that after all what happened the first face she saw after being in the accident was now letting her stay in his home. She was grateful. His wife puzzled her. She had been leading her all this time. But how did she appear and disappear like she did? Here she stood—alive—but when she saw her she was a spirit. She wanted to ask her, but didn't know whether or not Henry was aware of who or what she was. Hell, she didn't know who or what she was.

As she came to the dinner table and they blessed the food, Angelica's appetite came out. She hadn't really ate in days and it showed. They both smiled to see her eat, knowing that she was comfortable. Harry retired early—having to go to work early in the morning. Angelica helped Maria with the dishes. Before she could get out her first question Maria started talking.

"You have a lot of questions, young lady. And I have answers for you. I just wonder are you really ready for them."

"Who are you? You've appeared to me before my mother died in my room. At the bus stop leading me to what I needed to do. But you're here right in front of me—flesh and blood. What are you?"

"Many people have said that over the years. I'm just like you—in transition between planes."

"What? Transition between planes? I don't understand."

"I was told by a shaman years ago that when death makes a mistake that those people are left here until he finds his flaw and makes good on it. Before you and your mother came here to this town it was evil. The Petersons brought it here."

"But Peterson is gone. His wife still is living, but he's gone."

"And so is the evil—for a while. It seems to always rear its head up here. At least the books are destroyed. Your mother was a great help in helping me."

"My mother knew about this?"

"Not directly. You all coming was truly a blessing. Your mother was so strong. She helped me fight until her death. Took a lot out of me to keep your house from totally engulfing her. Shame that she had to die like that. But she has her wings and is on the right plane. We have ours, but death skipped over us. So I just believe that we're here until God sees for us to move on."

"I just want to go. So tired. All what's happened is too much."

"I understand. Not the first time this town burned like this."

"It's not?"

"No. First burned to my knowledge with me."

She went on to tell her about Old man Peterson and his son; how evil he had become, and his cult following. She sat there looking at her, and shook her head. "I'm so sorry for asking! They killed your parents?"

"Yeah. But when it came time to sacrifice me they wasn't able to kill me." She untied her scarf around her neck to show Angelica the scar—she had a scar from one ear to the other. "I never bled out. Then that's when it happened."

"What?"

"First the earthquake. I thought for sure that I would get swallowed up. But with all the commotion and people running everywhere to get out of the building, old man Peterson included, I was freed."

"So you made it out too."

"No, I didn't. Got caught under a huge rock. But they got it much worse than I did. That's when the fireballs happened."

"Fireballs?"

"Yes. Fire from the sky. I remember feeling the heat from them. I struggled to try to get from up under the rock, but couldn't I wanted to see what was going on. Somehow one of the members ran past me. I could smell the burning flesh."

"So how did you get out?"

"Fire and rescue. They dug me out. They said that both of my lungs were punctured, and all my ribs were broken. The rocks had broken a huge section of my spine. Scared the shit out of the responder when I asked them to get me out. Here I am, throat slashed from ear to ear, broken bones everywhere and I'm talking. He fainted!"

They laughed together. She was beginning to understand. It felt good to know that she wasn't alone anymore. That there was someone that went through what she did and understood. She asked about her husband's aura. "Why does Harry have a glow around him?"

She held her head down. "He's about to go. Only time I've seen them."

"Die? But he seems so healthy."

"He's not. He has cancer of the lungs. He won't take chemo—says that it does more harm than good. For a while he was on oxygen. Been helping him live his life. Drains me though. But I have to let him go. Death doesn't like to be cheated. I just pray that he takes us both. But I have a feeling that death doesn't want me anymore."

"He doesn't want me either if that makes you feel better. I know that I should have died in that accident!"

"No, I don't think it was a mistake for you. You wasn't supposed to be there. There was supposed to be another girl in your place. She got arrested a day before the get together. The Peterson girl just picked you at random."

"We all hung out."

"But she never really liked you. She just wanted to keep up appearances. The third girl had been sent off to girl's school. Her name was Trisha Goodall. She was supposed to be in the car—she was the third member of Alex's trio. She got busted for stealing—their sort of thing—and her parents sent her away. While in girl's school she stabbed another girl. When they asked her why she told them because she hated her "goody-goody" attitude. That sealed it for her coming out. The girl's parents demanded and got justice. Trisha is still doing the last of her time. She was far more evil than Alex could ever be. It was rumored that she was the illegitimate daughter of Marlon and one of the ladies in town."

"Wouldn't surprise me. He was really evil. I remember how he would look at Stasi."

"You know he paid Fannie to give him something to sleep with her?"

"Yeah, I read that among the letters my mother wrote. Delivered it to her parents. Her father was pissed. He didn't know. And the fact that he got her pregnant! That was the reason of them fighting that time before he died."

"You have any of those letters left?"

"Yes, quite a few. But some of these people have died, or they're hiding."

"Can I see?"

Angelica went and got the box. There were still 15 envelopes inside. As Maria looked through them she looked up. "Many of these people died in the fires. No other members of their family here. Going to burn them."

Maria burned 7 of the 15. She looked for her name. There was nothing there. Angelica looked up at her. "All these people were evil, or done something evil."

"I can hope. Just tired. Been doing this longer than you have."

Angelica held her head down. She felt bad to see Maria hurt. She wished that she had the answer she was looking for. "Why haven't you left here?"

"Can't. Tried. Seems as though whenever I try to cross that line to the next town I get drawn back, or something just turns me around. You wouldn't have gotten far either. We're stuck here."

Maria handed the box back to her and headed upstairs. Angelica looked at the box. *There you go! Now look what you've done! Why couldn't you checked before handing the box to her?* Angelica looked at the remaining names. She didn't know any of these people. Maybe Harry did. She would ask him tomorrow when she'd see him. She made her way to the bed they provided for her. She took in all what she learned today. It was becoming clear—she was there to take Maria's place. She looked up to the ceiling. How long had Maria actually been doing it? If she was a pre-teen when her accident happened, how old was she really?

Angelica looked at the names that were left over. She didn't know any of these people, and wondered with the two fires that had happened were they alive. She would start her quest in the morning. What Maria had told her about the Peterson clan made her wonder if his wife was truly innocent, or did she really know what was going on and went with it freely. She slept with more questions than answers.

Harry turned over as Maria came to bed. "What you all talk about? You didn't scare the poor girl?"

"No. Just told her that she wouldn't be able to leave this town if she wanted to."

Harry sat up. "Why you tell her that? She can leave whenever she wants! There's nothing holding her here. She's lost her only parent. She's alone in the world. How could you tell her that?"

"Because it's true. Just like I can't. Can you remember the last time you tried to take me outside of town?"

"That was just coincidence!"

"Your car's front end being smashed by nothing in front of it is 'coincidence'? What about the time when we had Allie and you tried to take me to the hospital in the next town? Remember what happened?"

"The car kept doing donuts and ended turned back towards the town."

"Exactly. You can leave, I can't. It's been that way for years. Even before I married you."

Harry looked at his wife. Maria turned over and went to sleep. *They were all coincidences*....but Harry remembered each time she was in the car it would do strange things. Even when they walked to the edge of town they weather would change, trees would fall, or the wind would almost knock them over until they changed course. What was Maria not telling him besides what old man Peterson was about?

The next day Angelica sought out to find Trisha Goodall. She wasn't too hard to find. She ran into her at the local McDonald's at the cash register. She eyed her over as she took her order and sat down to eat. Before long she joined Angelica at her table. "You're here for me aren't you? Going to take me back to jail?"

"No. You're the Trisha that Alex hung out with, aren't you?"

"Well used to hang out with before she set me up. Got caught doing something for her. Then she acted like she didn't even know I existed! Glad she's gone!"

"Are you really? The day before the accident she was telling Stasia that she missed you and that she was going to get you out that day."

"What happened? Bitch change her mind when another dick came along?"

"No, Stasia talked her out of it. Said that you knew what you were doing and to let your parents bail you out."

"I hated her. My parents couldn't afford the bail. I stayed there until the judge had mercy to let me go. By then she was dead. So all that time Stasia was telling her to forget about me?"

Angelica nodded her head. Trisha looked at her. "That's when I took your place. Alex couldn't break up her trio. But I could never take the place of you."

They both looked at each other in silence, before Angelica finished eating. Before leaving Angelica gave her the envelope addressed to her. Trisha looked at the envelope, puzzled. She placed the envelope in her pocket to read it later. Angelica went on to the bus stop. While waiting an older lady looked at her and smiled. "Your halo is showing. Might want to tone it down some."

"Not trying to show anything. No halos or wings. Just trying to deliver these letters my mother left. Not having a lot of luck. Just been able to deliver 1 so far. Lot of people lost in the fires."

"So true, but needed to be done. There's not a part of this town that hasn't seen those fires. I've been around a long time and I've seen about 6 of them in my time. Just waiting for my time here to be over."

"You can't leave here either?"

"No. Not until it's my time." As the lady stood up her mail fell. Angelica picked it up and noticed that it was the name on one of her envelopes. Was this lady evil? All the envelopes she had delivered were to people that evil or kin to people that were—minus Trisha who was supposed to have died in the accident. She looked at this woman—she had no halo or wings, just an aura. She looked at her funny.

"I know you see it. The aura. I'm the mother of Eric. You don't know me, but Maria knows me all too well. We were both part of Peterson's sacrifice. I was raped and left for dead—body thrown out in the trash to be burned. I was able to escape when the sparks of the fire started. Haven't been the same since. No man would touch me, and I have only Eric through what happened to me. Now he's gone. Fell prey to the evil of this town."

When Angelica gave her the envelope she cried. "Finally, I can go in peace." Angelica walked away, almost not by her own force to watch Eric's mother jump in front of the bus, her body making a loud thump as the driver tried to stop the bus. As the bus driver called for the ambulance and police, two cars sped by going in the direction of the McDonald's. Trisha Goodall had hung herself on the drive through pole. *What am I holding in these envelopes? Two people that committed suicide?* Angelica dropped the remaining envelopes at the bus stop and ran back to Maria and Harry's.

Charlie picked the envelopes up and tried to catch up with her to no avail. He looked at the names on the envelopes. He knew all of them—they were members of his family. He went home and made some calls. When all his family were gathered, he passed out the envelopes. When they read what was in them his sister asked him, "Where did you get these? We did this long ago! When old man Peterson was alive. I've changed Charlie. I don't do anything to hurt anyone. Who gave these to you?"

"A girl dropped these getting off the bus. There was an accident. The bus driver killed a woman. Hit her dead on."

"I heard. The deputy's mother jumped in front of the bus. The news just said another girl was found hanging in McDonald's drive thru. Who is this girl who dropped these envelopes? How did she know about what we did years ago?"

"I don't know who she was. She was by the bus stop. The sound of Eric's mother hitting the bus was deafening. The bus driver liked to have flipped the bus over trying not to drag her body."

"Where is this girl? Why did she deliver these to you?"

"She didn't! She dropped these."

"You should have left them there!" His siblings shook their heads in agreement. His brother Irwin spoke up. "She just gave us all our death sentences. This envelope tells everything I did while in old man Peterson's cult. No one else knows what I did but you all. Everyone else is dead or senile as hell. What does yours say?"

Charlie hadn't opened his up. Evading the question he asked Irwin what did his say. "What did yours say so bad? Like you said no one knows what we did! They're dead or either senile."

His sister spoke up, "Evidently not everyone has lost memory of that time. I'm not going to entertain this foolishness!" she tore up the envelope and walked out of her brother's house. Just then the weather changed. Fierce rains poured down. Charlie asked his brother was rain in the forecast. As they watched out of the window as their sister walked down the street to her parked car they saw it—lightening striking her right by her car. She was dead before she hit the ground. His other sister Marlene cried out in horror. "What the hell just happened? These envelopes are cursed! What do we do now? Who can remove this curse we you have brought on us?"

Irwin had read his aloud. "You are guilty of raping several girls, impregnating them, then killing them and their unborn children for the sake of evil. You lied, denounced God, and chose to serve the evil one and his disciple in hopes for eternal life that he could never give you. The blood of the innocents are on your hands."

His sister looked at him. She never knew exactly what he did in the cult. "Is that how you moved up the ranks?"

"Don't you dare judge me! You're not exactly innocent!"

"I didn't kill anybody!"

"Please!"

"I didn't! I bet my letter doesn't say anything about killing!"

"Then open it."

Marlene opened up her envelope and read it. "You are guilty of leading the sheep to the slaughter. You lied to so many young people about the empty promises of the cult—of the evil that was going to cost them their very lives. You stood by and listened to the pleas and screams of the young being killed for your leader to seal his bond with the evil one. You had the chance to change, but your sins multiplied when you attempted to kill the angel of deliverance sent to you."

"Bah! What damn angel of deliverance? All these envelopes are bullshit!" Irwin went into the kitchen for a beer. Marlene sat there in silence. She did know of who the envelope was referring to. She reflected back. She remembered back to a little girl named Marcia. She couldn't been more than 5 or 6 years old. She was brought to her to get her ready for service. Marlene couldn't bear subjecting the little girl to what was in store for her. There were men waiting to tear her apart—take her virginity and life for their and their leader's enjoyment. Not thinking clearly she attempted to kill the little girl, figuring that would be better than what was in store for her. Somehow the little girl escaped taking three other girls with her. She suffered being whipped before old man Peterson until she bled, which they took the blood from her that they would have gotten from the girl. She rubbed her wrists.

"Marlene are you alright?" Charlie asked.

"She's daydreaming. Trying to figure out a way to be more right than the rest of us. Ain't that right blessed sister? You and Greta make me sick. We did wrong and that was the top and bottom of it. Now you believe in a God that didn't do shit for you then or now. Pitiful. Charlie, if I drive you around can you show me that girl? I'll kill her off myself! That's how you end this shit!"

"You'll only die just as bad as our sister just did! It's a sign of repentance!"

"You can keep that shit! I'm finding that girl and kill her! Come on Charlie!"

Charlie was frozen to where he stood. He dropped to his knees for the first time in 50 years. "I don't want to die!" In disgust Irwin snatched Charlie's keys and left. Charlie and his sisters kneeled in prayer—praying for their very lives.

Angelica ran in the door almost knocking Maria over. She righted herself and looked at her. "What's the matter? Looked like you saw ghosts!"

"The envelopes....."

"You still have them? Or did you deliver them all?"

Angelica had no clue. She tried to focus to tell Maria of what she had witnessed. "Eric's mother....."

"I heard. You thought she was a good lady, didn't you?"

She cried in Maria's arms. "Most of the town was evil. As you see there are no children here. Whenever the women started to have babies the cult would rape and kill them all. So part of their curse was for all the women to be barren. There hasn't been a child born here in over 20 years. Alex, Eric and Anastasia were the oldest ones here to survive, but that wasn't how the curse worked."

"Who set the curse?"

"Fannie in part, for her brother failed to pay her for her services. Cursed him and his children. Everyone is gone in their family that stays here except his wife."

"But the other families? How did the curse spread to them?"

"At the last showdown Fannie had with those that opposed her she tried to curse their families. Saying that the evil one was more powerful than their god. Had many that day that had did blood sacrifices that day to give her 'power'. Back then we had several shamans here. They mostly stayed silent, keeping the auras of evil away from us that resisted the people who practiced it. There was one powerful one that Fannie wanted to take down."

"Did she?"

"Yes and no. Yes, she defeated him—but we say that he gave up his body for to reverse her curse toward us—and no, with his passing what she invoked to happen to us happened to all the members families that were there at the meeting. Over the years the evil came and went—we lost the last shaman when you and your mother came here. Your mother was good friends with her."

"I thought all shaman were men."

"Most are. Every now and then. However their wisdom passes down to their children. But not every child they may have may carry that blessing."

"How is that a blessing? I haven't seen any of this that has happened to me as that."

Maria walked off. Angelica hated when she did that. Why couldn't she just say what she wanted to and make things clear? Angelica wasn't going to follow her around like a lap dog today. She went up to her room to lay down. Once there she saw the book. She put the book aside, not caring about what it was about or reading it. She was through. This battle or whatever it was going to be Maria's and whoever else was fighting with her. Harry watched Angelica as she went up the stairs. He placed his coat over the hanger in the hallway and went to the kitchen where Maria was. "A bit too much history?"

"She needs to know what she needs to do here."

"For who Maria? Why don't you tell all of it to her?"

"I am, piece by piece. It's a lot for a young girl to take. How are you feeling?"

"Tired. But if I leave you now I know that you'll be taken care of."

She caressed Harry's face. Such a warm, caring man. Dying right before my eyes and all I can do is slow it down. Amazing how he's not afraid of dying—I'm tired, ready to go, but afraid. Have to teach this child for I can go on to the next plane. Harry kissed her hand and went upstairs. Maria looked out of the window when the phone rang. She picked up the phone, "We're coming to kill the bitch! We run this town as we always have!" then the phone went dead. Maria ran upstairs to try and wake Angelica up. She had locked the door. Shit!! She bammed on the door to wake her up. Angelica roused by the bamming on the door woke up and yelled "Leave me alone!"

"You need to get out of the room! They're coming to kill you!"

"Then let me die!"

"I can't! You're the last shaman! It's up to you to defeat the last of the evil ones! I'm not powerful enough!"

Angelica didn't move. *Last shaman my ass. We don't even have Indians in our family.* She was about to bury her head under her pillows when she heard the shots ring out. Whoever it was had arrived and was downstairs. She heard Maria slam the door and wake up Harry. Angelica walked to her window. They were everywhere. She heard one of them say, "There's the bitch in the window!" She came from the window and sat in the bed. She wondered were they going to kill all of them outright or do a ceremony to be able to put them on display. Whatever the case, she found herself calm....too calm. The room became very quiet and still; she didn't hear anyone else making noise in the house.

Maria heard the humming. Unable to move she told Harry to shield his ears, but it was too late. Harry had passed on. As the first two men entered her room it seemed as though they were moving in slow motion. She saw the flames. She was able to wrap Harry's body in a blanket from the bed and get him out to the ground with the last of her strength. She walked past the men who now wasn't moving at all to Angelica's room. Then she heard popping and splashing. She entered the room to see Angelica floating and spinning—the light so bright that she could barely look in her direction. She was in full form—something that she hadn't seen in over 40 years.

As she continued to rise Maria looked in her direction. It was her time. She knelt on the floor and gave her the last of her energy. With the last of her will she went down and laid by Harry and died. The men entered the house guns in hand. The heat in the house stopped them in their tracks. Then they saw it—Angelica in flames. Some of the men ran out of the house screaming; others were frozen in their tracks. As she walked past them they burst in flames. She went into Maria and Harry's room to see them dead. She looked at their bodies in disbelief. Her scream was heard from miles around.

Charlie and his sisters shook in their boots. It was beginning—just like the last shaman they killed told them it would:

"In your last days there will be a scream so shrill, so loud, so fierce that all will hear it from miles around. That will be the day of all the evil in this town to end. There will not be anything standing."

They prayed that they would be spared. Marlene stood up from praying and wiped her eyes. Her sister and Charlie looked up at her puzzled. "What's the matter?"

"She's coming. Can't you feel her coming? She's going to burn this town down like Sodom and Gomorrah! We won't get out alive!"

"She'll let us go. We didn't do anything to her."

"You were in on killing her mother! Have you forgotten?"

Charlie held his head in his hands and cried. "I don't want to die!"

Marlene's sister rose up and looked at Marlene. "My soul's good. I just want to ask her for forgiveness."

"Too late. Remember what the last shaman said to all of us before we killed him? The scream is the end of us all and this town. I'm ready. Evil has to end for good to thrive."

"I've done good! I've not mixed myself with all the sacrifices and murders! God knows my heart!"

"And he will judge us. For now, prophesy must be fulfilled."

Marlene walked out of the house closing the door behind her. She wasn't afraid anymore. She knew the damage she had done, and there was no amount of prayer that could change what she had done. She knew right from wrong, and she had opportunities to run, to change, to be like that girl that ran for her very life. She stayed—she learned to sacrifice others in order to do the minimum to stay committed to the sect. She even set her own sister up to be raped by 15 men to climb up the ranks. It was time for her to meet her maker, whether it was God or Satan himself.

As Angelica walked out of the house it went up in flames. Police cars screeched at the sight of her. Others in the neighborhood looked in terror. The police fired shots at her in fear, which exploded in air before reaching her. She looked around and raised her hands in their direction. Out of it came a fireball that consumed their car. The neighbors tried to run, but burst in flames as did the police and everything around her and in her pathway.

The fire chief saw the smoke from a distance. Some of the firemen got on their trucks and took off in the direction of the smoke. The fire chief walked back into his office. One of the other firemen went and got the chief's gear. "Saddle up! Got a raging fire to put out!"

"That's not a fire. It's the end of this town that no water can put out. You're running to your death. I'll stay here, drink me one more cup of coffee and smoke one more cigarette. Nobody will live past today."

The fireman took off, leaving the chief's gear on the desk. He pushed it all off, it was useless now. Vengeance was coming—and destroying all the evil once and for all. He looked at the color of the sky—it was brightly colored—some places orange and yellow, others blue and purple. The girl was strong. Maria must have gotten out, but not without giving her instructions on what to do.to every evil person left and the town. He decided to not take the coffee shot or the cigarette. He went into his glove compartment of his car and got his pistol. One shot it was over.

When the firemen went in the direction of the fires the wheels to the fire truck popped from the heat. They all saw it—the woman on fire walking toward them. They tried to get out of the fire truck, but the heat had bonded the doors. In minutes they were consumed. Angelica continued to walk on. The remaining people were running around trying to get away to no avail. They would all meet the same fate. They would all burn, along with this town. She walked onward to the cemetery. Marlene met her before she entered the cemetery. Angelica looked at her and stopped.

Marlene took a deep breath. "I did you and your mother harm. I want you to forgive me for what I did."

Angelica looked at her. She didn't ever remember her face being around either time the evil ones tried to kill her. She walked around her, as if she was checking her out. She began to speak again.

"Years ago this town was peaceful. Then old man Peterson lost his mind and turned it around. All the people that didn't want to follow him were tortured and killed. Back then there was a sect of Indians here. They never fought until provoked. Peterson wanted to be powerful like they were, so he killed them, drained their blood. He was powerful. But when he killed the last one a curse was placed on this town. No one that comes in can ever leave. It's like we're in a bubble. We exist, and for a while before the last shaman was killed very populated. When Fannie died she cursed the town again, not knowing about what we did earlier on to the shamans. She cursed all of us to die off and no more children to be born. The last shaman spoke of you. You are the angel of vengeance, retribution, and justice."

Angelica began to glow again. Marlene looked her in her eye, "I'm ready."

Angelica walked past her a few steps. "Tell the history of what happened here. Stay pure. Your last chance."

She walked past the cemetery to the other end of the town leaving flames and fires everywhere she stepped. Marlene looked at the fire ravaged town. Burning buildings, shells of people burnt to ashes. No trees stood, nothing green at all. The buildings were almost all gone. Marlene fell to her knees. She prayed that she would spare her sister and brother, but had a feeling that their day had come. She cried as the town burned all around her.

Angelica walked to the house where her life had changed. She looked at the house. *If I only obeyed my mother....*then she thought again to what Maria had told her. Still looking at the house she wondered if she would have stayed at home could all the death been prevented. Her head began to pound. She should have died and that would have put an end to all of this! As her tears fell she heard the low whirr. Then the screams. That shook her out of her thought to see the house in flames. Yet that didn't move her.

She found herself walking to the spot of the accident (by this time the whole town was fighting flames or people were trying to save themselves). It was just like yesterday in her mind. She could see herself jumbled in back of the car, in a place between heaven and hell. The tears kept flowing. She was all alone once again—or so she thought. As she looked in the distance she saw a figure of a person. Was it a man or woman? What are they doing all the way out here? What was she doing out here? She stood up and waited to see if the person was going to come in her direction. When they saw that they had her attention they stopped.

"Hey! Come here! I want to talk to you!" she yelled. The person didn't move. She got up to walk toward the person to talk to them about leaving here for their safety. As she started walking the person began walking toward her once again. She stood in place to see if this person was going to keep coming in her direction. No luck. They stopped. Why? She began toward the person again. They came toward her once more. As she got closer to her body felt cool—too cool. She stopped once more, about five feet in front of this person. By now she could tell that the person was a woman.

"Why aren't you running like everyone else? The town is on fire!"

The person didn't move or say anything. Angelica was beginning to wonder if see was seeing someone that wasn't really there. She decided to go on with whatever her business was that brought her there without the distraction. She walked in the direction of the other woman. The woman stood still. The closer she got to her the more Angelica felt cold. How could she be ice cold when her body was just on fire? She shook the thought out of her head and walked closer to the spot of the accident. About a foot away she stopped—the cold was unbearable. The woman was looking at her. When she spoke it threw Angelica off guard.

"Are you ready to go?"

"Go? No one escapes this town."

"Are you ready to go?"

"I've tried. Some type of barrier kept me here."

"I see you're not ready to go." The woman began to turn around and go back in the direction she came.

"Wait! Where do you want to take me?"

The woman looked back. "You're not ready. But you summoned me."

"I didn't call anyone! I don't understand what's going on! Please help me!!"

"To understand what your purpose is you have to accept it. Come with me."

Angelica followed the woman to the edge of the town. As she walked with her she noticed that all around her was burning to the ground. The sounds of people fading in the distance. Angelica wondered what happened to that lady she spared. The woman ahead of her stopped. "You are here."

"Where is here? There's nothing here!" Angelica looked around to see that she was alone with nothing around her. Where was the town? Was it all destroyed? Where had this lady taken her? She walked ahead, not knowing where she was going. She began to feel uneasy again, as if she was lead into a trap. All of a sudden she felt as though she had a great weight on her shoulders. She stopped in her tracks and sat down. Before long she was asleep. When she woke up she was surrounded my several men and women. Were they the shamans of old that had been killed? She was in awe of them all, and stayed on the ground. They all looked at her—plain faced, emotionless. A horn broke the silence scaring her half to death. The men and women turned and faced the sound. Mecca? What was so important about that horn?

She dusted herself off and turned toward the sound of the horn. As she looked she saw that she was in the midst of thousands of people. Had she died finally and was in the line for judgment? What was going on? After the horn the masses knelt in a wave-like motion. She was left standing, sticking out like a sore thumb. She tried to kneel, to be like everyone else, but found herself frozen in place. She felt awkward. Through the crowd she found out that she wasn't by herself. One by one those that were standing began to disappear. Her heart raced, what was going on? What was going to happen to her?

When her time came she was drawn into a light. At the end of the light she saw three people—a young woman, an old man, and a young man. She wanted to talk, but the words wouldn't come out. She began to cry. The woman looked at her, her eyes looked sad. The young man walked toward her. The old man sat down and watched the younger man make his way to Angelica. He reached out and touched her forehead. She felt funny, as if she was being electrocuted. She stood there in place looking at the young man. The longer he touched her the more the sensation intensified. The woman looked at her and smiled. Was she being tested or tormented?

As the young man kept surging power into her body she began to tire and wanted him to stop. As he kept on she began to return the power back on him with power of her own.

"She is strong. She has the markings." Said the young man.

"So much sadness in her eyes." Said the woman.

The old man just looked at her as the young man continued to rub her forehead and face, his touch electric. The woman began to smile. "She is one of us. She is the one that was lost."

The old man looked at the woman. "How did you come to that end? She was not born of our bloodline. She is not one of us." He signaled for the young man to stop. "That will not show us that she is shaman, for she is not."

The young man and the woman looked at him. "She's not?"

"No. Do her no harm. Who brought her here?"

"Wasn't she supposed to be here? She was in the town."

"She has a job to do from the high powers. Return her for she can finish. She is not ours to claim."

They did as they were instructed, returning Angelica to the site where she had met the woman. The screams and crackling of burning asphalt and metal woke her up. Behind her the town looked like a burning mass. The few screams were now gone. She stood there at the accident site all alone. She sat down waiting, trying to calm herself down. Then she remembered the books. During all the confusion she left them behind. She stood up and looked back at the raging fire when she heard another voice. "The books were not meant to be seen by man. They are where they supposed to be."

Angelica swirled around to see an angel. She fell to her knees.

"Rise, don't bow before me. You have served the master well."

"I don't know what to do. I have nowhere to go."

"There is nothing left for you to do. It's time for you to rest and be where you are supposed to be."

Angelica wondered about the woman she left alive. The angel answered her question. "She's dead. Even though she turned over a new leaf, she still has to stand before God to be judged."

"I know that I will be punished for all the things I've done. Just ready to go. Tired. Confused."

She angel smiled at her. "Then rest."

Angelica fell dead on the same spot the accident occurred a year before.

The town after the fire died down was left barren after the repeated fires and "paranormal activity." Nothing grew there, and no kind of traffic came near there.

When law enforcement came to the spot of where the town stood, they couldn't find anything that said that people had ever stayed there.

Years later when some developers tried to come in and build on the space where the town was, their building during the building process fell to the ground. People that rode through the old site of the town often would say that they saw Angelica on the side of the road whenever people would get lost, and that she would light their way. Angelica had finally got her wings.

Printed in the United States
By Bookmasters